Forged in Fire
By Chelsea Allen

ISBN: 9798836925949 (Paperback)

Library of Congress Control Number: TX 8-969-006

Any references to historical events, real people, or real places are used fictitiously. Names, characters, and places are products of the author's imagination.

Front cover image by Jaded By Design.

Printed in the United States of America.

Second printing edition 2022.

www.chelseaallenauthor.com

Prologue

You fear us, but you do not know us. You do not understand us. So instead, we hide in plain sight.

We are your mailman, your bag boy, your Uber driver, we are everywhere and nowhere at the same time. No longer having to hide in the shadows, we have come into the light and embraced the new age.

The new ways.

Magic is all around us every day, but people chalk it up to coincidence or luck, choosing to believe in logic over anything else. People fear what they do not understand, and we are no different.

No, we are the granddaughters of the witches you could not burn.

Mae

Mae Isobel Porter was born on January 7, 1668, in Salem, Massachusetts. She was merely twenty-four when the Salem Witch Trials took place and the strongest high priestess the Coven had ever seen in their history.

Year 2050…

"I can't breathe, I can't breathe… wake up Mae, WAKE UP!"

There I am, sitting up in my bed, my pajamas drenched with sweat. Heaving freezing air into my lungs, I look over at the clock on my bedside table and it is 3 AM on the dot. This is the fourth night in a row I have woken up like this, same time, the same dream, always gasping for air.

My curtain is blowing in the wind against the open window, and I hear the crickets singing their songs outside. I swing my legs over the edge of my bed and place my feet on the cold hardwood floor, and it feels so nice as the night air fills the room and starts to return my boiling body temperature to normal.

I walk over to the mirror and study myself, searching for anything reminiscent of my dream. I gaze over long, thick black hair, blue-grey eyes, and medium, curvy frame. I look at my arms, then down at my long legs, but find nothing out of the ordinary. No burns, no ash, nothing to confirm the nightmare was real.

I close my eyes for only a moment, and I am back *there*. I can smell the fire, the burning wood, and the black smoke coating my lungs. I can feel blazing fire licking at my skin as I struggle to loosen my binds against the stake, but it is no use.

And then it happens. The fire starts to engulf me, swallowing me whole, and I let out a blood-curling scream.

Suddenly I am back, bent over on my knees, trying to catch my breath for the second time tonight. My arms wrap around my waist like a vise, as tears stream down my face. It feels so real, even now, as I look around my room shivering from the cold. Remembering where I am and who I am, I steady myself and walk back over to the bed and sit down taking a deep breath in.

As I sit there the screams replaying in my head, the realization hits me, slowly at first, and then all at once. It is not a dream; it is a memory.

I was burned alive at the stake.

      *   *   *   *   *

At 9 AM my alarm starts to go off, time to start the day. I am groggy from lack of decent sleep as the memory of last night's dream haunts me once more.

I push the thought aside and climb out of bed, heading to the bathroom to get washed up for the day. It is an important day too because Genevieve Potts will be arriving at the bookstore today at noon to do her book signing, and she always brought big crowds and big crowds means good money for the shop.

Once I am dressed and done up to tackle the day, I head into the kitchen for my morning coffee, where Pumpkin sits on the counter waiting patiently for his breakfast.

"Good morning, Pumpkin," I say as he lets out a little mew.

"And happy birthday."

I kiss him on the head and pour him some hard food from the container next to him into his bowl. I head over to the coffee pot and turn it on, remembering I had already prepared it before going to sleep last night. Then something catches my eye.

There is a blue stone on the floor by the kitchen table, glimmering in the sunlight from the windows above.

I reach down to grab the stone when suddenly my phone rings and I jump, startled. It's Charlotte I think to myself without having to look at the caller ID.

"Hello?" I speak.

"Mae, you need to hurry down here, the line around the store is ridiculous!" Charlotte says her voice rushed.

"Ok Charlotte, I'm on my way, see you in fifteen minutes."

I hang up the phone and turn around to where the stone was, but as my eyes scan the floor, I see nothing.

It is gone.

I search around the table, underneath, but it is nowhere to be found like it was never there in the first place. I consider continuing my search for the strange, vanishing stone, but I look at the clock and it is already 10:36 am, making me late for work.

I quickly pour myself a cup of coffee, grab my purse and keys off the barstool, and head out the door.

Mae

I pull into the parking lot of Spellbound and cut the engine.
Three years ago today, I opened this shop, it just so happened to be
the same day I found Pumpkin. October is an incredibly lucky
month for me, it seems every good thing that has ever happened to
me manifested during this month.

Spellbound is not your average bookstore, it is also a
metaphysical shop specializing in crystals, herbs, tarot readings,
and more. The idea came to me one night and I just ran with it,
unsure if it would turn out successful or not.

After all, I did not know much about the industry, but
everything seemed to fall into place as if it was what I was meant
to be doing all along. The loan, the name, the location, and before I
knew it, business was booming and Spellbound was the place to

be. Not long after opening, we added a little coffee shop inside and customers loved it.

Coffee, books, and the occult who knew right?

But the biggest crowd drawer to Spellbound is when we bring in big-name authors on book tours to do book signings, especially when they are metaphysical authors, and today we have Genevieve Potts.

As I walk into Spellbound, the smell of incense flows through the shop. The bell attached to the door rings at my entrance, and Charlotte turns and greets me.

"Mae! Good, you are here. It's been crazy this morning and Genevieve will be here in an hour."

"Well then let's get started" I reply with a smile.

Charlotte heads to the register and starts to count the bills as I put my stuff down over at the counter. I gulp coffee before walking over to Genevieve's table she will be using today.

There are mountains of books surrounding the table and a large banner on each side with a picture of her. I straighten the papers on the table and ensure there are enough pens and bookmarks for her to use and then head back over to Charlotte.

"This signing will put us over the top in sales for the year" I laugh, feeling a buzz of excitement already.

"We could close the rest of the year if we wanted to, "she jokes before adding, "But you would never close Spellbound, it's your baby."

"You're right, I love this place too much," I say glancing around lovingly at my shop before switching back into business mode.

"Are we ready to open? Is the coffee shop prepared, register open, and extra books in the back?" I add.

"Yes ma'am, ready to rock and roll" she replies.

I let out a laugh at her enthusiasm and hug her.

"Thank you for always being here and helping run the store, Charlotte. What you do doesn't go unnoticed and I appreciate you."

"I love you, Mae. You're like a sister to me, and I've got your back. Anything you need, I'm here" she replies.

"OK, let's get this show on the road," I say, walking over to the door to flip the closed sign over to Open.

I swing the doors wide using the kickstand to keep it propped open and step outside into the perfect autumn air to greet the customers.

It is a beautiful fall day here in Salem. There is a slight breeze and a chill in the air. The leaves on the trees are red and orange and pumpkins fill the sidewalks of the bustling street.

As I step outside, I hug my coat around me and just stare in awe at the massive line of customers waiting to come into my store. I cup my hands around my mouth and begin to yell out,

"Good morning, everyone, and welcome to Spellbound! We are now open, please come in, get some coffee, and take a seat. Genevieve will be here shortly, so in the meantime feel free to shop around."

I step aside and let the customers pass me by, each one greeting me as they enter with a warm smile or a hello. I follow them inside the shop and head to the back behind the black velvet curtain where our backdoor is.

I take a seat at the table in the middle of the room, where there sits a crystal ball and some tarot cards. I light a stick of incense and set it down, as the smoke starts to fill the room, I take the tarot deck and begin to shuffle the cards. I close my eyes and take long deep breaths and focus on my happy place when suddenly there comes a knock on the door and I know it's Genevieve before I even get up from the chair. I walk over to the door and open it and welcome her inside.

"Welcome Genevieve, you're just in time. I was about to do a tarot pull if you would like to join me" I say.

"Oh wonderful," she says, "I'd love to."

We take a seat at the table together and chat for a few moments about the weather and what to expect for the book signing.

"Thank you so much for coming to my little shop, we had a line wrapped around the building this morning of your fans waiting to get in," I say.

"Oh please, anytime I come to Salem I have to come to Spellbound. It's a magnificent little shop and I love what you've done with it" she replies. "The energy in here is so pure and calming, and Mae you just create an atmosphere that draws people in. I can't explain it, but there is an energy around you, and it is pure magic. Have you studied your ancestry at all?" she asks raising her brow.

"No, actually I haven't. But I was born and raised right here in Salem. I've never been anywhere else," I reply honestly.

"Well, I think it's something you should explore Mae, and if you ever need guidance or support, give me a call. I'd be happy to help you on your journey."

I do not know what it was about the word journey or the look in her eyes as she says those words, but chills raced up my spine. Nothing malevolent of course, but something of mystery and wonder, like she knew a secret about me that was written clearly on my forehead, and everyone could see it but me.

"Thank you, Genevieve," I say.

"That's truly a wonderful offer and I appreciate it."

"Mae, it's 11 o'clock!" shouts Charlotte from the curtain, breaking my focus.

I look to Charlotte and then down at my watch. I had completely lost track of time, and we had not even done a tarot pull. I apologize quickly to Genevieve before doing introductions.

"Genevieve, this is Charlotte, my manager. Charlotte, this is Genevieve Potts."

I introduce the two ladies and they exchange pleasantries as I head through the curtain to the front of the store. I walk through the crowd to the podium we have set up for the signing and tap on the microphone twice.

"Welcome to Spellbound everyone! We are happy you are here, and we appreciate your patience. Now without further ado, let's give a big round of applause for Best Selling Author, Genevieve Potts."

Cheers and applause erupt throughout the shop, people are standing huddled around, and I even see a few tears of excitement in the crowd. I step down off the podium and Genevieve comes through the velvet curtain and through the crowd to stand next to me.

She steps up to the microphone, "Thank you Mae for the introduction, and thank you for having me in your wonderful shop today. I can't say enough how grateful I am to be here in Salem with all of you and how excited I am to kick off this book tour right here in Spellbound!"

Genevieve pulls up the chair set out for her, and everyone takes a seat and quiets down. I sit down behind the counter with Charlotte as we listen to the reading excerpt of Genevieve's new book, *Unbound* as my mind starts to drift.

Mae

"On a farm in Mississippi, isolated from the prying eyes of the townsfolk, was a little girl running through the corn fields, frolicking, and dancing around with her doll.

"Anne! Come inside, it's getting dark," shouted her mother.

"Coming mama," Anne shouted back, darting for the house as fast as her legs would take her.

Anne came barreling through the front door as her mama held it open for her.

"Go wash up for supper," Tabitha said, as Anne ran up the stairs to get ready for dinner.

"Hello darlin', how was your day?" Andrew said to Tabitha as he came into the room, taking off his hat.

"It was fine dear," she replied. "However, I sure did miss you."

Andrew walked over to Tabitha and grabbed her, spinning her around, dipping her backward, and then kissing her softly but deeply. They were the epitome of true love. Just then Anne came jolting down the stairs to see her parents kissing.

"Ewww gross," she said.

They both stopped and laughed as Tabitha replied, "Ok now, let's all sit down to a nice supper."

After dinner, Tabitha and Andrew put little Anne to bed and headed to their alter room in the attic. As they opened the door, hundreds of white candles burst to life and lit the room, illuminating the darkness and chasing the shadows away. Tabitha and Andrew entered the room and shut the door behind them, walking to the center of the room and sitting down on the floor, taking each other's hands. As they began to chant, a cold breeze swirled through the room, flipping the pages to their grimoire that sat between them. Suddenly, the spirits of hundreds of ancestors appeared around them, filling the room, and bringing light energy to the home.

"Why have you summoned us?" the elder asked.

"Anne's thirteenth birthday is at midnight, and she comes into her powers. We need the amulet," Tabitha replied.

"The amulet holds great power Tabitha and must be used for light magic only. Has she chosen her side?" the elder asked.

"She has," Tabitha replied.

"And she's going to birth the most powerful daughter the Coven has ever seen. She'll be High Priestess, I've seen it."

"Then the amulet is hers," the elder replied, manifesting an amulet in her hands, and handing it to Tabitha.

"Take great care with this, for it's the future of our line and the only way she can summon the ancestral line. But I must

warn you, there is a great threat on the horizon for Anne's

daughter, and only she can stop it." the elder said.

"We will," Andrew said and just like that, the ancestors

disappeared as quickly as they appeared.

"Mae? Mae! Are you ok?" Charlotte asks me, shaking my

shoulder.

"Yeah, I'm fine, sorry drifted off for a second, just a

daydream but I'm back," I laugh, getting up and walking over to

the counter. Unsure of what I just saw, I shake it off and get started

on the massive line waiting at my register.

Mae

I am ringing up book purchases when Charlotte hands me the phone, saying I have a call.

"Who is it?" I ask.

"They just kept saying 'It's me,'" she replied.

I give her a weird look, then take the phone from her as we switch places. Charlotte continues ringing up purchases as I slip into the back room to take the ominous phone call.

"Hello?" I ask.

"Who is this?" I press.

"It's me" the raspy voice replied. "Mae Isobel Porter and I were burned alive at the stake."

Suddenly goosebumps run up and down my arms and I start to panic.

I can't breathe.

The air is being pulled out of my lungs and I drop the phone to the floor.

It bounces with a thud against the hardwood floor and falls to pieces. I can feel an asthma attack coming on, and I bend over, with my head between my legs, gasping for air, begging for this episode to end when Charlotte walks in and runs over to me.

She has my inhaler in hand, and she places it in between my fingers and helps me level it up to my mouth and press down, releasing the medicine into my lungs.

I take a few deep inhales followed by some deep breaths, and the attack starts to subside, but that feeling of panic still sits heavy in my chest.

Charlotte walks me over to the table and sits me down in the chair, taking the seat across from me. She grabs my hand and holds it, rubbing my palm with her thumb, trying to comfort me.

After what seems like an eternity, I calm down and my breathing returns to normal.

"How did you know about my asthma attack?" I ask her.

"I just had a feeling you needed it. It was strange," she replied. "What happened? Who was on the phone?"

I took a deep breath and a moment to think of how to respond. I couldn't tell her the truth; I would sound insane. It all seemed crazy even to me, it can't be real, the dreams, and now this.

"It was just a bad prank call. You know how kids are this time of year." I lie.

Charlotte takes it at that and does not press me anymore on the issue.

"Well, if you're okay, I'm going to head back up to the front," she says.

"Ok, I'll meet you up there in just a second," I reply.

She gets up and disappears through the black velvet curtain and I lay my head down on the table for a few minutes, counting down from one hundred to ensure I have my bearings before I head back out to face the bustling shop full of customers.

It's 5 o'clock when the last customer leaves for the night. Normally we stay open until 7 pm but with it being such a big day, I decide to close the shop early so we could go home and get some rest. And after my panic attack earlier, going home and lounging in bed with Pumpkin with some Netflix does not sound half bad.

"Thank you for your help today, Charlotte, you were amazing in more ways than one. Oh, and do not worry about setting up the new till, for the register, it can wait until morning. Just go home and get some rest, you've earned it."

"Thank you, Mae, it was quite the day. I'll see you in the morning," she says, turning and walking out the door.

Once she left, I walked over and turned the sign in the window to Closed and locked the door. I started back towards the counter to grab my purse and keys and then reached under the register to grab the money from the day to take to the bank for a deposit.

That is when I felt it.

Smooth and cold, not perfectly round but solid, and immediately I knew what it was without having to see it.

The mysterious blue stone that had vanished from this morning.

*   *   *   *   *

I sit on the couch, coffee in hand with the computer on my lap open to Google. I slowly turn the stone over and over in my right hand, lost in thought about its appearance earlier this morning, and then again at the shop.

Could it be connected to my dreams? Or even the phone call I got this afternoon? It seems like it's all one big dream that I will wake up from any moment now.

I am running the day through my mind when suddenly the doorbell rings and makes me jump. I set the coffee down on the table and push the laptop & stone onto the couch and get up to answer the door. I open it to see a small brown package on my porch, with not a single person in sight.

Curious, I take the package inside and head into the kitchen, grab a knife from the drawer, and cut the top open. Inside the box is an aged leather-bound journal.

I open the front cover and there written in cursive in the top right corner is my name, dated January 7, 1683, my fifteenth birthday.

How can this be? Who sent this? Where did it come from? Why is my name on it? A thousand unanswered questions race through my mind at lightning speed.

At this point, my head is swirling with confusion. With all the events that have been happening lately. Can they all be connected?

I grab the journal and head back over to the couch, put the laptop in my lap, and start to scour the internet. I am not sure what I will find or where to even start, but all I know is that I need answers.

And I need them now.

I start with my dream and search, '*Mae Isobel Porter burned at the stake*' and '*Mae Isobel Porter 1668 Salem, MA*'. Nothing comes up for what I am looking for.

I try numerous other searches and combinations with no success until I give it one last try and type in '*Mae Isobel Porter Salem MA witches 1692.*'

There it is. I stare at the screen and for the first time today, my racing mind is speechless.

It's me.

Well not quite me, but a woman that could be my twin.

I scroll down to find a short story about her being the High Priestess for the Salem Coven in the 1600's. I read on to find that they were the most powerful Coven of the time but a peaceful one and together they protected the people of Salem.

It wasn't until the Salem Witch Trials that it became unsafe for them to practice and many of the coven members lost their lives when one of their own turned them in after having gone dark; Tituba.

Mae tried to fight Tituba for the sake of the Coven and the people of Salem, but the darkness was too much and overwhelmed her power. Mae was discovered as a witch and burned at the stake on October 22, 1692, today's date.

I studied the picture of Mae for several minutes. Her eyes, the curve of her lips, her long thick black hair, it was like staring in a mirror. But most importantly, the amulet that sat upon her neck, felt familiar, like it was calling to me like I have worn it before.

A faded memory starts to suck me in when the phone rings.

I snap out of it and set the laptop down and get up to get the cell phone out of my purse. I answer but no one's there, there's just silence, and after several seconds the line disconnects. Probably a spam call.

I think nothing of it until I head back to the computer to finish reading about Mae when the search result is gone. I refresh the screen, I retype my search, I go through my browsing history which comes back empty, I try everything, but that page never comes back up.

Like it never existed at all. It seems everything has a knack for vanishing today, I think frustrated as I slam the computer shut and lay back on the couch. I grip the blue stone in my right hand, retracing its curves and edges that seem so remarkably familiar.

That is when sleep takes me over.

Mae

"Mae Isobel Porter, you are accused of witchcraft and are sentenced to die by fire. Do you have any last words?" the mayor says.

I say nothing, as I look out over the crowd of on-lookers and there I see her, Tituba, with a wicked smile upon her face.

"May God have mercy on your soul," the mayor continues as he lights the kindling and sets the stake ablaze.

I can feel my heart threatening to beat out of my chest.

'Save yourself' it cries, every urge in my body wants to fight to stay alive. But instead, I use my precious time to whisper a reincarnation spell under my breath. It would not save me from the pain I was about to feel, but I knew I had memorized it for a time such as this, it would ensure my return.

I would not let Tituba win and I would finish this war that she started. As I get the last of the words out of my throat, the blazing fire seers my skin, the smell of burnt flesh settles in my too-hot lungs and I let out a scream that would be my last. Suddenly the entire pyre is engulfed in flame, and I am burning.

I wake up in a panic, my lungs burning for fresh air, drenched in sweat once more. I look over myself searching for signs of burns or ash that must be there, only to find nothing.

I look over at the kitchen clock and it reads 8:16 PM. I slept for one hour. Just then Pumpkin mews and jumps up on the journal that is sitting on the coffee table. At first, I think he is playing with the cover, but then I realize he is trying to turn the pages. Odd, but not the weirdest thing that had happened today.

I pick him up and place him in my lap, grabbing the journal and searching for the page he was pawing for. Anything is possible at this point.

And then I feel it, a bizarre warmth coming from one of the pages, as if it was calling to me, I flip it open It is a memory spell, to recover lost memories.

Something in my chest sets fire and a feeling of belonging settles there, I was meant to read this.

I have to read this.

I can't fight the pull it has on me and without thinking I recite the words written carefully on the page.

"Across the dark and starry night,

I seek what's lost to come to light,

bring forth what has been lost to me,

restore my forgotten memories."

Bright lights burst from the pages, swirling around me ferociously. The air gets thinner, and I am wrapped in a whirlwind, and I cannot fight. Memories fly past me, swirling like a storm, and it feels like a dream I have forgotten, just out of my grasp. I reach my arm out, stretching towards the images, from a life I can't remember. I am lost in this swirling mass for what seems like an eternity until suddenly, it happens.

It is like I am a computer, and the memories are being downloaded. They hit me like a ton of bricks all at once with a painful surge to my forehead. It feels like I am splitting open at the seams as decades worth of life, force their way into my brain. One more surge of inexplicable pain, and suddenly it's gone, as quickly as it came.

No more whirlwind, no more flying memories, and no more pain. But something is different, I am different. I am no longer just Mae, bookstore owner, I am Mae Isobel Porter, High Priestess from 16th Century Salem.

Pumpkin jumps into my lap.

"Hello old friend," I say as I lift him for a kiss. "It has been a long time."

You see, Pumpkin was my witch familiar in 1692, as was reincarnated into his current form when it came time to find him. Everything started falling into place and the puzzle pieces began to fit together, I felt oddly complete. Like part of me had been missing and I couldn't quite put my finger on it until this moment.

Today was the anniversary of my death in 1692, nine days before Samhain, or Halloween as it is known in 2050. The stone, the journal, the dream, and the phone call, it was all clues to awaken my memories, to awaken myself and to accept myself entirely.

My spell worked the night I was burned, and I have reawakened in a whole new century. A century where magic is real and was once embraced but as history repeats itself, the use of your powers now gets you persecuted. I see not much has changed after all. Most importantly, I have not forgotten that I still have an enemy out there determined to wipe me out once and for all, Tituba.

Mae

As I work to catalog the memories that are swirling inside my head, I decide to brew myself a cup of chamomile tea to calm my anxiety. The last thing I need right now is another panic attack today.

I take a sip and can feel the warmth running through my body. It has been ages since I have had tea, but it seems fitting tonight. I start to flip through my journal, a gift I was given on my fifteenth birthday. It holds my most powerful spells, memories, and thoughts from the age of fifteen to when I died on the stake at twenty-four.

I am thirty-two now in this life and I have accomplished so much I feel pride for both lives that have now fit into one. I graduated with my Business Degree and opened Spellbound, without any idea what I was doing. Once business started booming,

I was able to upgrade my tiny one-bedroom apartment to a three-bedroom house in The Village. From there, other things just worked out and fell perfectly into place. Some people call it luck, I call it hard work and manifestation. If you visualize what you want and focus on it daily, it will happen for you.

You just have to believe it.

As I snap back to reality, I remember the journal. I was looking for a spell. But not just any old one, the very one that would recall my powers to me. As I turn the pages, memories come flooding back to me from my childhood, growing up in Salem in the 1600's, before the witch hunts began. It was peaceful and serene. My family was a prominent one in the community, unbeknownst to everyone that we were the most powerful witches Salem had ever seen. But we hid it well. We attended church with the others, and kept to our responsibilities within the community, secretly healing and helping the townsfolk when necessary.

We were their protectors, but they would be our demise.

My father was a doctor and my mother, and I were all well-kept. We lived in a large colonial home right in the center of town. If I looked out my window at night, I could see the gallows where guilty men hung, but we did everything we could to protect the people of Salem.

We were an active part of the community, and we would heal the sick and dying with potions and natural remedies. We kept Salem alive, and it worked for many years until Reverend Cotton Mather went on a witch hunt and 4 little girls decided to stir the pot and put on a show no one would ever forget.

Once the trials began, Tituba was among the first to be accused. But to save herself she sold out the Coven, and me by giving my name specifically, and the rest was history.

Or so she thought anyway.

Suddenly I am jolted back to the present. My hand is hot like it has just touched a flame. I look down and there it is in front of me. The spell, and I recite the familiar words,

"Stuck within a day and night

searching for my birthright

bring to me what has been lost

bring back my powers at any cost"

My power hits me square in the chest.

A force stronger than any I have ever encountered, and it knocks me backward, flat onto the floor. I am writhing in pain, my veins are pulsing threatening to burst, my heart is racing, and I'm gasping for air once more. My head is pounding, I feel this pressure pushing inside and it is unbearable. I can't hold it in anymore, the pain is excruciating so I scream. A piercing, sharp scream, one I remember.

I feel like I am dying, and that makes me panic more. I gather the strength and crawl over to the journal, where it landed a few feet from me on the floor.

With every ounce of strength I have, I pull myself forward, dragging my lower half behind me, reaching my right arm out for the book, when suddenly everything goes dark.

I black out, thankful to feel the pain fade with my vision.

Mae

When I wake up, sunlight floods the house, and I can hear birds chirping outside. I look around and see that I'm on the kitchen floor, the journal a few inches away from me.

I slowly sit up and go to reach for the journal, but when I stick my hand out, it comes to me instead, part of me is surprised I wasn't even aware of real magic until the other day, and the other part of me is relieved.

The spell worked. My magic is restored.

As I get myself up off the floor, there's a knock at the door. I'm slow to steady myself, but once the room stops spinning, I head to answer it. Again, there is no one but a package left. A gift box sits alone in front of my door, beautifully wrapped in shiny blue wrapping paper with a blood-red bow on top. The tag on the corner says "Mae."

I grab the gift and head back inside the house, locking the door behind me. I set the gift down on the counter as I go for my cell phone on the coffee table.

I dial Charlotte. I tell her I'm not feeling well and ask if she can take care of the shop today.

Not quite a lie, but not the whole truth either.

"You sound really strange Mae. Are you sure you're, okay?" she asks me.

"I'm sure, I think it's just one of those 24-hour stomach bugs," I tell her.

"Hopefully, I'll be better by tomorrow."

"Okay, just get some rest and feel better," Charlotte says before saying goodbye and hanging up.

I set the phone back down and walk over to the kitchen counter where the mysterious gift is sitting. I cast my sense out but strangely I can't get a reading on it. Strange, but then again, I haven't had my powers in decades.

I start to peel the wrapping paper off to reveal a brown box. It's not sealed, rather the tops are tucked underneath one another. I open it up and out swarms thousands of black flies, hitting me in the face, enveloping me in chaos, their buzzing so loud I can feel my ears bleeding.

There are so many that they're heavy on my skin and I barely move. Struggling to get them off, to be able to hear, and see. Trying to be free of this swarm that is attacking me. But I'm frozen in place. I try to raise my arms but I'm still so weak from last night but with every ounce of strength left in me I raise my hands and manage to scream,

"BANISH!"

My body goes slack, the buzzing stops, and the flies are gone, like it never happened. I take a few deep breaths and steady myself and look inside the box.

Inside is a note with no signature. It says, "I'm coming for you," and instantly I know exactly who it's from, Tituba.

Her essence is all over the inside of the box, I can feel her dark magic oozing out of the corners.

It's just like her to send such a message.

I can feel myself start to weaken even more, dizziness setting in. I steady myself on the counter for a few moments until I have some semblance of strength. I grab a glass of orange juice from the fridge and head into my bedroom. I take a few sips of my juice and set the glass down on the bedside table and then climb into bed.

It feels like ages since I've laid in my bed and after sleeping on the hardwood floor last night, it's nice to be on a down comforter. I snuggle up underneath the blankets when Pumpkin jumps up and curls up beside me. I pet him a few times and rub behind his ears, as I close my eyes, letting a gentle and peaceful sleep wash over me.

I wake up around 3 pm and I'm sore. Magical attacks are brutal, not to mention my collapse last night. I get out of bed and walk into the bathroom and grab some Tylenol from the medicine cabinet. I take two pills and wash them down with some tap water.

I look myself over in the mirror and I look wretched. Makeup smeared, hair knotted, clothing all wrinkled, I look so much older than I felt from being drained; I need a shower. As I turn it on and wait for the water to heat up, I get undressed. That's when the bruises catch my eye.

I'm covered in them, from my shoulders to my ankles. The flies squeezed and battered me, and I didn't think anything of it because I was so tired, but now black and blue bruises adorn my porcelain skin.

No wonder I'm in pain.

As I step into the shower, the warm water hits me and at first it hurts, but then it starts to soothe my tense muscles and aches and I relax, drifting into a conscious meditation. I clear my mind of the attack and the pain, and I let myself drift away into my safe place, my happy place, where I can recharge and heal.

But most importantly, I can plan.

I'm in a forest and I can smell the pine trees surrounding me. There's a cold breeze blowing and crickets chirping nearby. I can sense animals all around me, grazing and sleeping. Above me a beautiful owl graces me with its presence, and the largest and brightest full moon I've ever seen and around it is a blue ring.

The full blue moon.

I'm sitting on the forest floor, grounding myself with Mother Earth, enjoying my surroundings, the sounds, and smells, all of my senses working, and finally finding some semblance of peace and balance.

I can feel my Chakras opening and my energies aligning, and I feel nothing but happiness, complete pure happiness. I visualize all the negative energy and thoughts leaving my body in a black wave as positive white lights flood in.

I get up off the forest floor and start to dance underneath the full moon, swaying with the breeze and moving to the music of the crickets. I can feel the grass and twigs beneath my feet as I move to the beat of my own drum.

It's safe here.

There's no one allowed here but me.

But I can't stay here forever, I must get back to reality.

I take three deep breaths and open my eyes, and I'm still standing in the shower, hot water running down my back. I look down at my body and the bruises are gone, as is the pain I was feeling.

After my shower, I get changed into some clean pajamas and feed Pumpkin. I make myself some dinner and settle onto the couch to watch a little Netflix and relax. Once I finish a small dinner of frozen pizza, I try flipping through Netflix trying to find something to watch but I can't get Tituba's warning out of my head.

She's coming for me, and I must prepare.

I must find a way to stop her. Black magic vs Light. The ultimate battle. I find myself terrified she's already been the death of me once and has managed to attack me now that my powers are back.

But how did she know?

I didn't tell anyone about the journal or the weird clues I was getting yesterday. No one was here when I recalled my magic.

Or were they?

     *   *   *   *   *

Tituba used to be my best friend since childhood. The daughter of a murdered slave, we took her into our home, and she was raised as one of us, as my sister, my equal.

It surprised the community, and many thought the great Doctor had lost his mind, but they trusted him and his judgment for he never led them astray before, so soon the people of Salem came to accept Tituba as part of the Porter family.

Tituba was raised on our beliefs and light magic. She practiced the art even though she didn't appear to have any gifts herself. That is, until she turned thirteen. Suddenly everything changed. Tituba became darker, meaner, and more aggressive, and the biggest change was when we found her levitating above her bed one night, surrounded by black light.

Tituba came from a Santeria tribe in Africa where Voodoo was in her blood and triggered at the age of thirteen. One day we came home and found the family cat butchered and hanging from the stair railing. Tituba said the cat scratched her and had to be punished. There were other instances as well, but we don't talk about them, for fear of awakening the demons she summoned, and we fought to shackle.

As she got older, we kept her inside the house more and rarely let her outside. She didn't participate in community events anymore, nor did she do her simple outdoor chores.

When the witch trials began, Tituba began acting strangely. She was eating more, and sleeping longer, and always locking herself in her room for hours on end. Little did we know, Tituba was doing this because she needed her strength.

To what end, we never found out, but with me out of the way, I couldn't stop her anymore. The day before my trial, she snuck out and retreated to the woods. She reappeared to give her testimony and then disappeared shortly after. I didn't see her again until hours later when I was burned, with that haunting, wicked smile splitting open her face.

Tituba had accepted the darkness that had been chasing her all her life, and I was the price she had to pay.

One she paid willingly and without a second thought.

Tituba

I felt it when Mae received the journal from her spirit guides, and I knew she would be recalling her powers soon after. It was time for me to send her a message.

I am here but you won't be for long.

But little did she know, dear old sister was closer to her than she thought. All it took was a glamour spell and to her I was Charlotte.

Her friend, her ally.

The woman who had her killed all those years ago.

When Mae was reincarnated, I decided to stay close, because I knew this day would come. The day when one October, the memories of her death would be strong enough to awaken her and trigger the spell.

Then last night it happened. I was in her backyard, watching through the open curtains when she recited the spell. I watched her blackout and saw the white light of magic flood into her, like a hurricane in a small town.

And I knew the time was close. Now with seven days to Samhain, Mae's time is running out.

I took on the persona of Charlotte, Mae's manager at Spellbound. I remember the day she put the ad in the paper for help wanted. And many were interested. But I cast a spell to ensure no one would show up, all but handing me the job on a silver platter. Mae immediately liked my skills and experience as a prior bookstore owner as she personally had no experience, though she would never tell anyone that.

I had many references and a degree from Dartmouth in literature. There was no way she could pass me up, she'd be a fool. Luckily, she didn't verify my resume, because of course, none of it was true, although, with a few words I could make anything true, so I wasn't worried. And just like that, I went to work for dear old sis. Biding my time and playing the devoted friend. And she never suspected any different.

There was a close call yesterday however when she got that phone call. It spun her into a panic attack, and she needed her inhaler. I could feel her panic spread through my body. I could feel her gasping for air and her airways closing tight so I grabbed her spare inhaler from under the register and took it to her.

She was no use to me if she was dead. It was too soon, and all of this would have been for nothing. So, I played it off and said that I just had a feeling she needed it. She didn't seem to think anything of it or question my intentions, she was just thankful I was there when she needed me the most.

As I watched her puff on the inhaler and regain her breathing, I couldn't help but feel a tiny twinge of guilt. She was my sister; she took me in, and we played together as equals. But as we grew up, they denied me my true self, my birthright. They tried to alter my magic and dim my darkness. I was born Tituba, Voodoo Queen and no one was going to take that away from me. So, in secret I practiced dark magic and explored who I was and truly meant to be.

I had help from Madame Laveau and Papa Doc who trained me in their wicked ways and taught me everything I needed to know. I danced with the evil spirits at night and summoned demons to do my bidding. And ultimately, I betrayed Mae and watched her burn to fully embrace my powers.

I don't regret it.

Mae will be suspicious of everyone in her life, anyone coming into the shop, maybe even Charlotte, as she tries to find me. I have a shield around myself when we're at the shop together and I'm portraying Charlotte so she can't sense anything.

I wouldn't want to get caught too early and spoil the surprise I have coming for her. There's a battle coming, one of light and darkness and we're going to finally find out which is stronger. I've waited over three hundred and eighty-two years for this moment and nothing is going to spoil it.

I will destroy Mae once and for all and plunge Salem into darkness.

Mae

Suddenly the phone rings and I know it's Mrs. Williams from down the street.

"Hello?" I answer.

"Yes, hi Mae, this is Mrs. Williams. I just wanted to call and check on you and see if everything was alright. A group of us gals went by the store today, but it was closed, and I can't ever remember a time when Spellbound has been closed," she says.

"Closed? Are you sure? Because I asked Charlotte to run the store for me today since I wasn't feeling well," I tell her.

"I'm sure my dear. Dark as can be and not a person in sight. But I sure hope you feel better, and we'll see you back open soon, take care and bye now," she says and then disconnects the line.

Closed? Where was Charlotte today then? If she couldn't run the shop, why didn't she just call me? So many questions were swirling around my mind trying to make sense of it all.

I dial Charlotte's number, but it goes straight to voicemail.

Odd.

I try the shop but the line just rings and rings. She didn't even turn the voicemail on for the shop. Panicked, I get dressed and decide to head to the store to check things out. I grab my coat and keys and I'm out the door in a flash.

After 15 minutes, I pull into Spellbound and there's not a vehicle in sight. Just a single light post that is flickering as usual. The shop looks okay but I won't know for sure until I get inside. I get out of my car and walk slowly up to the door. I test it, and it's unlocked.

I open the door and reach inside to the left and flip the switch for the lights, illuminating the dark shop from every corner. I brace for the impact of a robbery or worse, but everything looks the same. Nothing is damaged and nothing appears to be missing or out of place.

Then I smell it, fresh incense coming from the back room.

"Charlotte?" I call out.

No answer.

I walk to the black velvet curtain and pull it to the side, on the table is the crystal ball and a fresh stick of incense just lit, and a Tarot spread.

"Charlotte, are you here?" I call out once more.

Silence.

I cast out my senses but feel nothing. Just the chill outside, the static of electricity running through the air, but nothing else. I walk over to the back door and check to see if it's locked, and it is.

This is getting strange.

As I turn back around, three Tarot cards are flipped face-up, revealing their artwork. They weren't like that a minute ago.

Feeling uneasy, I put my shield up to protect myself from an attack, just in case. I visualize hot blue flame surrounding me, protecting me, and I start to feel all warm.

It's working.

I walk over to the table and sit down and look at the Tarot spread before me.

I see The Devil, The Tower, and Death.

Bile rises in the back of my throat, and I fight the urge to not be sick. The ominous message rips through my mind like a tornado.

"There's a battle coming, one unlike you've ever seen or experienced before Mae and it's going to destroy you if you let it. Family is the key to your survival. Be wary of those around you, someone is not who they pretend to be, and they will be your demise. It's in the darkest of times that we find out who is truly there for us and who isn't Mae, never forget we're always with you."

Just like that, the pain is gone, and tears are streaming down my face.

"Mom," I whisper into the darkness of the room.

It was my mother's voice.

She was giving me a message through the Tarot cards. And there, sitting on the cards is my amulet from 1692. All black filigree design with a Lapis blue stone in the center. It's one of a matching set, Tituba has the other.

I put the amulet around my neck and fasten it. And I can feel the power of my ancestors flowing through it.

It's an immensely powerful relic that I can summon my powers through and the powers of all my ancestors before me. I look at myself in the mirror on the wall behind me, admiring the beautiful glimmering stone when suddenly something catches my eye.

The section of dark magic books that we store in the back is missing a few volumes. I know they were here yesterday, and we don't sell those, they are purely for collection, even Charlotte knows that.

Then it hits me, Charlotte's phone is turned off, she didn't actually open or close the shop, two black magic books are missing, and the other day she just knew I was having a panic attack and happened to have my inhaler at the ready. As I make this realization panic overwhelms me and images flood into my mind of Tituba glamoured as Charlotte.

Tituba knows where I live, she knows my secrets, my doubts, my fears.

She has been running this shop with me for years.

My own sister, my best friend... right under my very nose and I had no idea.

Why didn't she just kill me when I reincarnated? Save the trouble of having to play the part of Charlotte for so long.

What's her end game?

…The amulet.

She wants our powers, and she must take them through a living descendant. Her amulet wouldn't work good magic anymore, it would only do dark magic and evil. That's why she's kept me alive. She needed me to recall my powers and find the amulet.

She wants to plunge Salem into darkness, it's all about power and control for her. She's been watching me, waiting, living a lie to get close to me. Suddenly I feel sick and run to the bathroom.

My dear sister, what aren't you capable of.

    *   *   *   *   *

I walk in the front door and toss my keys on the kitchen counter. I'm exhausted but the shop is locked up tight and my amulet is safely around my neck. Three hundred- and eighty-two years Tituba's waited for me and held this grudge.

I can't believe it.

Her Voodoo powers must've made her as close as an immortal can get, for her to live this long. And she's had centuries to practice her dark arts and refine her magic. I've had one with my magic back.

There's no way I can fight Tituba alone and win. Feeling defeated, I head to bed. I have a battle tomorrow with Tituba, and one of us isn't going to be walking away from it alive.

Mae

It's 5 AM when I wake and there's a heavy energy looming in the air all around me.

It's time.

I get out of bed and quickly get dressed in my black cargo pants and blue tank top. I pull a sheer white top over my tank and throw my hair up into a high ponytail. I grab my combat boots and lace them up tight.

I'm ready.

I look in the mirror and my amulet glimmers in the light. I touch it and can feel the warmth of light and goodness within. I walk over to my bedside table and grab a thick yellow envelope from the drawer, holding my will, the deed to my house, and other important documents to be found if I don't survive.

I kiss Pumpkin on the head and fill his cat bowl before I head out the door.

"If I don't come back Pumpkin, you know to find your next charge right," I ask him.

He looks up at me with sad eyes and mews, rubbing his head against my shoulder.

"I love you Pumpkin," I tell him as I kiss him on the head.

At least… should I die again; I get to say goodbye this time. Tears fill my eyes as I remember the fact that I wasn't able to the last time.

I grab my keys and coat and I head out the door. As I drive down the block, I stop at the mailbox, holding the yellow envelope in my hands.

Tears start to stream down my face as I drop it into the mailbox but it's going to my lawyer, and I know she'll protect my assets and do the right thing with what's requested of her. I jump back into the car and head to Spellbound.

As I pull into the lot, it's still dark outside. There's not a single light on inside the shop either. I'm here first. I climb out of my Jeep and start to walk towards the door. I take three deep breaths and insert the key into the lock and pull the door open. Once inside I flip the lights on and lock the door behind me and head to the back room. Everything is quiet. The Tarot cards are back in a stack, the incense is long burnt out, and there's a calm in the air, like a calm before the storm.

I pull the chair out from the table, and I sit and wait. I pull my shield up as blue flames lick up and down my skin, encasing me, protecting me. I cast my senses out, searching, waiting.

Then I hear it, the lock on the front door clicks and the bell above the door jingles.

Tituba's here.

A hand reaches around the curtain and pulls it to the side, revealing Tituba in all her darkness, not having aged a bit. She's wearing a long black dress with blood-red strips running down the sides. She's wearing her amulet, a black filigree design with an Amethyst stone in the center, only there's a swirling fog of evil protruding from the stone.

It's like watching a thunderstorm, with lightning strikes touching down and deep purple clouds coating the sky as thunder rumbles deep within the heart of the storm. I'm lost inside the stone for what seems like an eternity when my amulet starts to feel hot on my skin and brings me back.

"Stay back," I shout, holding my hand out as blue electricity hits Tituba in the right shoulder.

She winces in pain and fires back as a bolt of purple shoots past my head, a little too close for comfort.

"We don't have to do this dear sister," I say.

"Oh yes Mae, we do," she replies hitting me square in the chest with both electrified hands.

I fall back to the ground, clutching my chest, trying to catch my breath. Tituba moves toward me, and I drag myself to hide on the other side of the table. My lungs feel as if they're on fire as I try to take in a shaky breath.

"Without your inhaler dear sister?" She asks menacingly.

"How were you the prodigy of our coven, the strongest, the most regaled when you can't even breathe?" she continued.

"You're weak Mae, you've always been weak and now you will pay the price."

Tituba walks around the table, holding her right hand out in the air, making a tight U shape with her fingers, choking me with her magic. I kick and move around, trying to get out of her grip, but it's no use. Tituba has me and she knows it.

I'm going to die.

Everything starts to go dark, my breathing slows down, and I can feel my soul weaken.

Just as I'm about to stop fighting, a white light shoots out of my amulet and into Tituba, striking her in the heart and knocking her backward. She loses her grip on my throat and must use her hands to catch herself from falling to the floor.

I mouth a quick healing spell I learned in childhood because I know I only have seconds before Tituba regains her balance. I can feel my lungs opening, my throat healing itself and, at that moment, I feel stronger, more powerful than I have in days.

I take the opportunity and throw a spell at Tituba, tossing her in midair against the far wall of the shop. As she hits the floor, she lets out a vicious hiss.

"So, you want to play dirty. Then we'll play dirty sis," she says.

Out of her hands shoots two bolts of purple electricity but I block it with my shield. It bounces off the shield and hits Tituba in the shoulder, knocking her to the ground. As she gets up, she wipes blood from her lip and charges at me, full force, knocking me down to the ground with her.

Tituba is straddling me, taking a swing at me with magical force. Trying to subdue me. But I catch her fist in my hand, and with all of my strength I use my right leg to lift her and throw her off me collapsing onto the ground in the corner of the room. Thinking I had knocked her out. I started walking towards her, when she waved her arm and threw me hard against the wall. Feeling the fire within me I counteracted with a huge blue energy ball, which knocked Tituba back to the ground.

"Enough of this!" she screams.

Tituba rips the amulet off her neck and holds the stone out in front of her. She starts speaking in tongues as her eyes roll into the back of her head. Her body starts to convulse and as she starts to levitate off the ground and into the air. Dark fog surrounds her, and demons start to escape the amulet, chasing one another around the room. The chanting is so loud that my ears start to bleed, and I'm brought down to my knees, unable to move.

"Demons of Darkness, Do. You. WORST!" Tituba screams as she throws her arms out, still levitating midair.

Just then an explosion rocks the room, and there's a ringing in my ears, blood trickling down my face.

Suddenly there's glass everywhere. And I'm bleeding all over. I feel heavy and trapped but I can't see anything, it's all gone dark.

I can barely breathe, I can't move, but I feel like I'm spinning in circles when finally, I pass out.

The windows in the front blow out, the door is ripped off its hinges, bookshelves are in pieces and books are fluttering around in flames.

The shop is destroyed. No one could have survived this.

The townsfolk would be told it was a gas leak from the inside coffee shop to avoid any suspicion of witchcraft. The shop would be closed and have to undergo lengthy renovations, thank goodness for insurance.

As for Tituba, she would make her escape that fateful night, leaving behind no trace of her destination. She would leave believing that she killed Mae, succeeding in the first part of her plan to plunge Salem into darkness.

But for Mae, her story is far from over.

The spell rocked the entire building, destroying the bookstore. As Tituba levitated back down to the ground, she tried to find Mae to see if she had succeeded in killing her, but with an explosion so loud Tituba knew people would be here any second and she had to get out. Deep down she knew there was no way Mae could've survived, so with a wicked smile upon her face, she opened a portal and quickly jumped through, leaving Salem behind her.

Mae

I wake up to the sound of sirens and people yelling my name. Everything was unsteady, my vision blurred and a ringing in my ears.

I tried to pull myself up off the floor, only to fall back onto my knees when a pair of hands grab me and sweep me up into their arms. The fireman carried me out of the shop as I waned in and out of consciousness, my eyes darting around what was left of my store.

The last thing I remember was being placed on a gurney in the back of an ambulance as he told me I'd be okay, the doors quickly closing, and everything going black.

3 days later…

The hospital room is a bright white, the kind you see in those awful movies about psych wards. There isn't a pinch of color except for the awful turquoise curtains that hang over the window on the far wall and the matching plastic couch that sits underneath it.

There are flowers all over the room from the townsfolk and various customers with cards wishing me well and some rainbow balloons tied to my table, bringing some joy to the otherwise lifeless space.

I have been here for three whole days, being poked and prodded and having every test possible run on me to ensure they weren't missing anything.

After the explosion, I lost a lot of blood and had to have a transfusion. All the broken glass had cut me open like a Turkey on Thanksgiving, leaving me with stitches all over my body. The doctor said I was incredibly lucky, minus the blown eardrum, a concussion, and some fractured ribs, but it could've been much, much worse.

As far as I know, Tituba doesn't know I am still alive, or else she would have come for me by now, so I have to be incredibly careful about using my magic so she can't track me.

I know time is not on my side, but I have had a least a few days to devise a plan to defeat Tituba, once and for all

It won't be easy; I will need all the help I could get and that meant summoning my parents from the spirit realm, but first I have to get out of this retched hospital and back home.

By noon, the doctor comes in checks my vitals for the hundredth time and draws more blood.

"When can I get out of here and go home?" I ask him.

"Well, if your blood work comes back fine and your vitals stay steady, I can discharge you today, Mae, but you have to go home and take it easy. You are on mandatory bed rest for 2 weeks, no exceptions, do you understand?" he asks.

"Yes, I understand, thank you," I replied as I shoot him a weak smile.

He places my chart back down and walked out of the room, closing the door behind him.

I lay back on my pillow and took a deep breath, sleep overtaking me and my weakened body.

A few hours later, the doctor comes in with the discharge papers and Mrs. Montgomery, my neighbor.

"Hello dear, how are you feeling?" Mrs. Montgomery asks.

"I'm okay, just tired and sore," I reply to her.

"Well, your blood work came back perfect as did your vitals so I'm sending you home Mae, but remember what I said about bed rest," the doctor speaks.

"Of course, cross my heart and hope not to die," I chuckle.

He looks at me, unamused, and goes back to signing the papers. Mrs. Montgomery helps me out of the bed and grabs my clothes from the bureau as I head to the bathroom and got dressed, more than ready to bust out of this place and never look back.

Ten minutes later, we were in the car and headed across town to my house. Mrs. Montgomery is going on and on about her book club and her gardening but I'm not listening, my mind is elsewhere as I look out the window, watching the city pass us by.

"Mae are you okay?" she asks me finally.

"Oh, yes I'm okay, sorry I drifted off," I lie.

"Oh, that's ok dear, it's to be expected after everything you've been through. I mean a gas leak in your wonderful store, how on earth…but thank goodness you're alive, that's what matters. Ah, we're here," she says.

I look up and we're in my driveway, I must have been completely zoned out in thought because I didn't even know the car had come to a stop.

"Thank you, Mrs. Montgomery, I appreciate the ride home. You're a life saver," I tell her.

"It's not a problem dear, I'm always happy to help you. Let me get your suitcase and I'll meet you at the door."

I slowly climb out of the car and grab the keys from my purse and head for the front door. I unlock it as Mrs. Montgomery comes up behind me with my suitcase, swinging open the door and stepping inside, turning off the alarm that's fixed on the wall, right inside the doorway.

I grab the suitcase from Mrs. Montgomery and place it inside the doorway and thank her again for the ride and for looking after Pumpkin for the last few days. "It was truly my pleasure dear. Pumpkin is such a good kitty; he makes it so easy. Now if you need anything at all, just give me a holler," she says.

"I will, thank you so much," I respond as she turns and heads back to her car.

I close the door, locking it behind me, and set the alarm. I head deeper into the house, calling for Pumpkin as I walk into my room, tossing the suitcase onto the bed, and collapsing beside it.

Just as sleep was about to overtake me, Pumpkin jumps up next to me and starts to purr, rubbing his head against my arm.

"Well, hello old friend," I say. "Did you miss me?"

Pumpkin answers with a mew and continues rubbing against my swollen body.

"I got lucky Pumpkin, but I need to prepare quickly, because Tituba is coming for me sooner than later and this time one of us won't be walking away again," I say to him.

As I scratch his head, I roll over to my side and close my eyes, letting the stress of the last few days dissipate as I welcome the sweet escape of my dreams.

Tituba

I am back at Auntie's house, having left Salem behind me in a rush. I can't believe it; dear old sister is dead, and I can move forward with my plans.

Auntie Laveau and Papa Doc meet me at the door, in what I assume to be a celebratory greeting, only their faces seemed drawn and disappointed. Certainly not the look I was expecting from them after what I had just accomplished.

"Hello little one," Papa Doc greeted me.

"You put up quite the fight, didn't you?" he says.

Confused, I nod but stayed silent.

"However, it was not enough Tituba, Mae is still alive," he continues.

"No, that's not possible, I destroyed the shop, there's no way anyone could have survived that," I say outraged.

"Come, my dear, let us show you," Auntie says as she heads inside, leading the way for us to follow.

Once inside, Auntie leads us into the den where she keeps most of her supplies. On the table in the far corner is a crystal ball, with a white mist floating around inside of it.

Auntie simply points toward the crystal ball and says, "take a closer look my dear, and all will be revealed."

I take a step closer and peered into the glass ball, staring at the mist. After several moments, the mist dissipates, and images become clear. And then one came into focus; it is Mae in the hospital, injured but alive.

"How!" I shouted.

"How is this possible? I used every ounce of power with the decimation spell, she should be in pieces. This is simply not possible," I continue.

"The ball is never wrong my dear. She was wearing her amulet; you can see it on her in the vision. It must have protected her from certain death," Auntie said.

"But this is not the end Tituba, it's merely another opportunity. Mae will be more prepared this time around, but so will you. This time you'll have Papa Doc and me to help you," she adds.

A wicked smile crossed my face and I know she is right. There was more power in numbers and Mae was outnumbered.

Dear old sis was in for a surprise, I hoped she was ready for it.

Mae

I wake up the next day to the sound of birds chirping outside my window. I completely slept through yesterday, but I was so exhausted and in so much pain it was to be expected.

I look over at the clock on my bedside table, noticing it said 8 AM. As I turn back around, I see her standing there at the foot of my bed, Tituba.

Only it wasn't her, she was projecting herself from wherever she was. I let out a deep breath I didn't even realize I'd been holding as Tituba began to speak.

"I see you're still alive dear sister, but not for much longer. I hope you're ready for me because this time I have a surprise up my sleeve and there will be no escape for you," she says.

"Get ready Mae, I'm coming for you in 3 days."

And just like that, she is gone.

It took me a few moments to collect myself; Tituba knows I am alive, and she is coming. I don't have much time; I have to start preparing if I am going to beat her once and for all.

I climb out of bed and head into the bathroom, turning on the shower, and giving it time to heat up.

As I take my clothes off, I see all the stitches and bruises covering my swollen body. There's no way I can fight in this condition, so I close my eyes and picture my forest, my escape. I call upon my ancestors and spirit guides and ask for their healing powers to flow into my body and mind. I can feel the sound of the shower start to drift away as I'm taken away to my forest, where I can meditate and be at peace.

Twenty minutes later I come to and I'm on the floor of the bathroom. I must have passed out when calling forth all that healing energy, as I'm still pretty weak after all.

I get up and look at myself in the mirror and all the bruises and stitches are gone. In their place is perfect porcelain skin. "Thank you," I say out loud as I climb into the steaming hot shower, so glad to be out of pain and able to properly prepare for battle.

After my shower, I get dressed and grab my cell phone out of my purse. As I sit at the foot of the bed, I contemplate calling her because I don't know how much she knows or if she'll think I'm crazy, but there's something about our last interaction that just tells me she can help me.

I take out the business card from inside my purse that has Genevieve Potts's information scrolled on it as I start to dial her number.

Genevieve meets me at the local coffee shop in town around noon, just a few miles from Spellbound. I find her at a table in the back where we'll have privacy from prying ears. I walk up to her, and she embraces me in the biggest hug I've ever had, and it feels so nice; warm and comforting.

"Hello dear, I heard about the accident, are you okay?" she asks me.

"Oh, I'm okay. It's actually part of why I wanted to talk to you today. I need your help with something. Something big," I say.

"Well sit down dear and let's get to it," she says.

"You know, for someone who was in the hospital for 3 days after an explosion, you look mighty well to me," she inquires suspiciously.

"I was healed by my ancestors this morning. I called upon their healing energy, and they granted my request," I say.

I take a deep breath in and slowly exhale, preparing myself for her reaction, expecting her to call me crazy and laugh in my face.

Only she looks at me with nurturing eyes and responds,

"Well, I'm not surprised Mae. Your ancestors are your protectors, and you have a battle in 3 days' time. They weren't going to let you go in fighting weak and injured."

I was so stunned I think my jaw hit the floor.

"How did you know?" I ask her.

"Mae, I'm a witch too, from a long lineage of Salem witches. I know your story well, as it has been told from generation to generation. I knew you'd come back in my time, and I was overjoyed when I got to meet you at my book signing, even if you hadn't regained your full memories yet. The ancestors have been talking and you Mae are in grave danger and need all the help you can get if you're going to defeat Tituba," she said.

"How can you help me Genevieve without putting yourself in danger?" I ask her.

"Oh, don't worry about me dear, this is your story, not mine. And our destinies are already written. I'm not scared of death Mae, I'm scared of Tituba reigning over Salem and harnessing the ancestors power, so I've gathered every available witch in Salem to come to your aid, they'll be at the bonfire tonight in Mead Park at 10pm to meet you and prepare," she said.

"That's wonderful Genevieve, I'll be there. How can I ever repay you for your kindness?" I ask.

"Just defeat your sister Mae, and keep both light and dark magic in balance," she says, giving me the warmest smile and taking my hand in hers.

Tituba

The projection worked. Mae received the warning.

I'm sure she is in panic mode, injured and weak, trying to practice with powers she's only had back for a week now.

As I toss the final ingredient into the potion, it explodes with a large puff of purple smoke.

It is ready.

The potion is going to call upon the Powers of the Damned to help give us each a boost in power for the battle. As I pour the potion into three glass vials, the dancing demons sway across the walls of the den, swirling in tune with the jazz music playing on Auntie's record player.

I've been practicing my Voodoo incantations and my magical combat spells all day with Papa Doc. Even the decimation spell seems much stronger this time around, as I lay ruin to Auntie's home on the bayou, but luckily with magic, it was only temporary. As I cap the last vial, a portal on the far wall began to open and out steps Auntie, cloaked in black velvet with red heels.

"How is the potion coming along my dear?" she asks.

"I just finished it and capped off three vials for each of us," I reply.

"Wonderful. Now it's time for you to rest Tituba. You've been at it all day and you need your strength. That's an order," she commands.

Auntie rarely ever gave me orders, so I knew there was no way out of this.

"Yes ma'am," I say, as I gave my wicked smile and headed to the guest room down the hall.

*   *   *   *   *

Madame Laveau waits until Tituba shuts her bedroom door to uncap the three glass potion vials. She takes a needle from her pocket and pricks her index finger, dripping a single drop of her blood into each vial.

She shakes them up to ensure they mixes properly and shelves them in the cabinet on the wall.

"What Tituba doesn't know won't hurt her," she mutters to herself as she walked out of the den and into the kitchen.

Mae

Around 9 PM I grab my keys and head for the door.

The bonfire is starting in an hour and all the witches of
Salem would be there. It is nerve-racking but also so exciting to be
around so much good magic.

I climb in the Jeep and start her up, old reliable. I pull out of
the garage and head for Mead Park across town. As I drive down
the dark deserted highway, I couldn't help but think about what I
am going to say to these women.

How am I going to inspire them to join forces with me to
stop Tituba? Afterall, it won't be easy, and many will potentially
lose their lives along the way. I don't have the answers, so I just
kept my eyes on the road and drove.

As I pull into the parking lot of Mead Park, I can't help but feel anxious, when suddenly it hits me like a cool breeze on a hot summer's day.

The magic in the air, it is intoxicating, inviting, and more importantly, good. I can feel it like static electricity, running along my skin like a thousand little pin pricks. They are here and they are gathered already. I follow the flow of magic to a clearing surrounded by beautiful pine trees, where a large bonfire rages in the center of it all. There, circled around the bonfire are hundreds of fellow witches, holding hands and chanting, casting a protection spell around them.

As I walk up to them, I am careful not to break their concentration when Genevieve approached me.

"Hello dear, I'm so glad you could make it."

"This is amazing Genevieve. There must be three hundred witches here," I exclaim.

"Well, three hundred and fifty-eight," she replies, "but who's counting," she says as we both laughed.

"Come, join the circle, Mae. After we finish our protection spell, I'll introduce you to everyone," she says.

I follow her and join in, chanting a spell as old as me, but one I knew quite well.

After several minutes pass, the protection spell is cast, as it is a cloaking spell so no passerby's can see us. Genevieve walks into the center of the circle and welcomed all the ladies, thanking them for coming tonight. It is then that I realize, it is my turn to talk, and I am definitely not prepared.

I suck in a deep breath and join Genevieve in the center of the circle.

"...let's all welcome Mae Isobel Porter," Genevieve says as an eruption of 'welcome' and 'blessed be' comes from the crowd.

I stand there frozen, with hundreds of pairs of eyes on me, unsure of what to say. Minutes of silence pass in what felt like hours, when I finally open my mouth to speak.

"I struggled the entire drive over here with what I was going to say to you amazing ladies. Many, if not all of you know who I am and my story. You know I was burned at the stake in 1692 because of my traitorous sister Tituba, who has been free over the centuries, while I just regained my memories and powers in this life a week ago. Tituba wants to destroy Salem and bring darkness to reign over the people, and she has the power to do so. I have to stop her, but I can't do it alone. Good magic must prevail over Salem and the world, so I'm here to ask you ladies for your help. It won't be easy, some of you may lose your lives along the way, but it's for the good of Salem and the future of good magic. It's for your children and their children, and all the generations to come. So, I'm asking you, will you join me?"

Suddenly an eruption of cheers and applause breaks my focus, and I can't help but cry. I was dreading that they'd say no but the witches of Salem will not stand for dark magic, let alone have it reign over their home.

They're going to stand with me, and I don't have to do this alone.

A weight lifted off my shoulders and I just smiled. I walk through the circle and hug every single woman there, thanking them for their help and sacrifice. There is a light at the end of the tunnel, a legitimate chance that Tituba can be defeated, and it feels so empowering.

As the bonfire festivities carry on, Genevieve and I separate from the group and sat a little bit away for privacy.

"Now Mae, what do you know about your amulet?" Genevieve asks me.

"Well, my parents gave Tituba and I a matching pair when we were younger. The only difference is the stone in the center. Mine is Lapis and Tituba's is Amethyst. I've always just harnessed my powers through it to amplify them when I needed it the most," I replied.

"Mae, the ancestors gave your grandparents that amulet when your mother turned thirteen, knowing that one day she'd pass it onto you. It's for so much more than harnessing your powers Mae, because with it, you can harness the collective powers from all your ancestors before you, giving you essentially endless power," she said.

"The amulet also allows you to call upon your ancestors, bringing them back as spirits if you need them. The amulet is the epitome of good magic Mae, you must protect it with your life," she continued.

"Why didn't my parents tell me any of this?" I asked her.

"According to the ancestors, they were waiting until your twenty-fifth birthday, but Tituba interfered when she named you as a witch, killing you before you could be warned. They wanted you to enjoy as much of your life as you could before you had to worry about some prophecy coming true. They were simply protecting you, whether it was the right thing to do or not," she said.

Tears start streaming down my face, I miss my parents so much.

"I wish I could talk to them again Genevieve, just hear their voices one more time," I say.

"Oh, but you can Mae. Just use the amulet," Genevieve says.

With a simple smile, she reaches over and hugs me, it's warm and comforting.

"It's getting late my dear, I must be heading home. I'll see you the day after tomorrow. Get some rest, you're going to need it," she says, as she turns and walks away, heading for her car.

*   *   *   *   *

The bonfire carries on until sunrise, but I leave shortly after Genevieve once I say goodbye to the ladies. I come home and go straight to bed, I was so exhausted after learning everything I did last night, but I was glad I did. I needed to know.

The next morning, I rollout of bed around 10 AM and immediately start a pot of coffee. I only have about an hour until I had to leave for Spellbound, as I was meeting the construction workers there to go over the plans for the repairs and renovations. Luckily, the insurance kicked in quickly so I could get the shop back up and running sooner rather than later.

I drink my coffee as I got dressed, trying my best to multitask. I quickly run a brush through my hair and head into the kitchen, tossing a Pop tart into the toaster and pouring some coffee into a to-go cup. As soon as I heard the toaster pop, I grab my breakfast and head out the door. As I climb into the Jeep and started her up, I pull out of the garage, waiving at the mailman as he walks by. I pull out onto the street and start on my way to Spellbound.

When I arrive, the construction crew has already begun the clean-up process, removing the wreckage from the shop, and tossing it in the dumpster outside. I carefully enter the shop and look around for the foreman, David, as I feel a tap on my right shoulder from behind. I jump and let out a little scream as I turn around to see it was David.

"I'm sorry," I say.

"A bit jumpy this morning, aren't we?" he asks with a chuckle.

"Just a bit. How is everything going?" I ask.

"Well, we have the clean-up underway, and then tomorrow we'll begin the repairs to the structural damage. That'll take about a week and then we can begin the renovations and get your shop back to looking as beautiful as it was before," he replies.

"That sounds great. Do you have the blueprints for the new design?" I ask.

"I thought you'd never ask," he chuckles.

As David and I look over the blueprints, I can't help but feel a twinge of sadness, as I may never get to see my shop finished if I don't win this battle tomorrow.

After talking to David about the plans for the shop, I decide to stop and get some lunch at the local diner in town. A cheeseburger is calling my name, I just can't say no. After I ordered, I decide to check my emails, it has been days since I have been on my phone.

Nothing too important, just insurance stuff, order confirmations for the shop, etc.

Then I check my social media, logging onto my business page for Spellbound, posting a status update,

'Clean-up is underway. There's going to be a new Spellbound in town.'

I scroll through my newsfeed, checking up on my friends when my burger is set down in front me. I thank the waitress and dig in. I continue to eat and scroll through Facebook for what seems like hours. I even toss in some Amazon shopping; I have Prime free delivery after all.

It's nice to just sit and do something as stupid and trivial and eat a burger and sit on my phone and not have to think about what's looming on the horizon tomorrow. I'm as prepared as I'm going to be, so right now I'm going to enjoy myself and just breathe.

I get home around 5 pm, Pumpkin greeting me at the door with a happy little mew. I bend down and pet his furry little head, scratching behind his earns like he loves. I scoop him up and carry him with me into my bedroom and set him down on the bed.

I grab a few white pillar candles from around the room and make a circle on the floor. With a few simple words, they burst into flame, illuminating the darkening room. I walk into the center of the of the circle and sit down cross-legged.

With one hand on my amulet, I say,

'Bring to me my family lost,

reunited at any cost,

their divine wisdom I must use,

or else this battle I will lose.'

Everything illuminates with swirling lights, a cool wind blowing throughout the room. The candles blow out and a bright white light forms in my doorway. After several moments, the lights dull and suddenly the room is filled with hundreds of spirits; my ancestors.

I look around, so blessed at the scene before me that I start to cry.

The elder steps forward and says, "hello Mae, it's been a long time."

I study the elder for some time, noticing that I have her eyes, the same long black hair, and simple smile.

"I'm your great, great, great…let's just say I'm your VERY great grandmother Agnes. My, it is so good to see you. We've watched over you your whole life, but it is a pleasure to be summoned by you," she says.

"I know you have a lot of questions Mae, so let's start at the beginning."

"Can I talk to my parents, Agnes?" I ask.

"They're right behind you," she says with a smile.

I turn around and there they are, my father's arm wrapped around my mother.

"Mom, dad…I've missed you both so much," I say.

"We've missed you too Mae," they reply.

"How could you not tell me I'm part of a great prophecy concerning Tituba? Don't you think I should've known so I could've been better prepared?" I ask.

"I mean, Tituba is so strong, she's been around for centuries. How am I supposed to stop her?"

"You're not alone Mae," my mother says.

"You've got the power of the witches of Salem behind you, not to mention the collective of the ancestors."

"But how do I tap into the collective?" I ask her.

"You simply focus on love Mae. Love is the key to unlocking the power, and once you do, you'll be stronger than your sister, there's no doubt about that. You can do this Mae, you have the will, and you have the power," she says.

"But I'm scared mom," I tell her honestly.

"I know you are Mae. But you are not doing this alone," she responds.

"Now get some rest, tomorrow is a big day."

Tituba

Papa Doc and Auntie are waiting by the gates of the Underworld for me, when I portal in, holding the three vials of potion.

"Are you sure this is going to be enough?" I ask.

"Yes, my sweet, this potion will amplify our joint strength by giving us the Powers of the Damned. Every power that is displaced when the Underworld takes a new victim, gets harnessed into a collective called the Powers of the Damned. Only those that know how to access it can use it, and we are going to share it today to defeat your sister, Tituba," Auntie replies.

"We will have the force of the Underworld at our backs, Mae won't know what hit her."

A wicked smile crosses my face as the end is in sight. Victory for me and Salem in my grasp. I hand Auntie and Papa Doc each a vial, and we each consume the potion, armed and ready for battle.

Auntie opens the portal as the three of us step through and into Mead Park.

Mae

Thunder begins to rumble as lightning strikes the sky, illuminating the darkness. I can feel the electricity in the air, biting along my skin like a million fire ants.

There's a heaviness in the air, a thickness that feels like it's almost suffocating; Tituba.

I feel it when she came through the portal, everything changes. The sky darkens and it begins to storm, people on the street are more aggressive and argumentative, and I can feel the darkness oozing into the corners of the town.

She is here and she is ready for a fight.

I knew she'd be at Mead Park; it is the most private and easiest to cloak from outsiders. As I drive towards the park, the rain comes pouring down in buckets, pounding down on my Jeep.

My windshield wipers are moving as fast as they could go but it is still impossible to see anything. I pull old dependable over and put the hazard lights on, jolting out of it and running across the street. If the Jeep can't get me there, my feet certainly would, it is less than a mile away.

As I approached the park entrance, I stop to catch my breath when a spell caught me off guard and hit me in the right shoulder, sending me flying backwards onto the concrete.

"Hello sis, you're looking mighty well for someone who's supposed to be dead," Tituba says.

"I could say the same thing about you," I reply sarcastically.

Tituba lets out a maniacal laugh as I roll onto my side and dodge another one of her attacks.

"Oh, I hope you don't mind sis, I brought a few friends to the party," she said, sneering.

I looked up to see Madame Laveau and Papa Doc come out from around a huge Oak tree.

"Not fighting fair as usual I see," I say.

"But unfortunately for you, I brought some friends too," I say.

Just then the entire outskirts of the park were lined with three hundred and fifty-eight Salem witches, creating a circle, encompassing us.

"You're smarter than you look sister, I'll give you that," Tituba says as she shoots another fire bolt my way.

I dodge the attack and run deeper into the park, as the Salem witches have Madame Laveau and Papa Doc occupied. Tituba chases after me, throwing spells and fire bolts at me as we run. As we hit the clearing, I come to a stop and throw my hands up, throwing Tituba through the air. As she gets up, she starts to chant, but I hit her in the arm with a spell, throwing off her concentration.

Blood starts pouring down her arm and I know this battle was far from over.

"We don't have to do this Tituba," I yell over the storm.

"Oh yes dear sister, we do!" she screams as she runs at me full force.

I throw a magic right hook at Tituba, and it knocks her off balance long enough for me to cast a shield around myself.

"I will not let you destroy Salem Tituba, this is not your home, it's mine and I will protect it with my life," I say.

I take my hands and form a circle with them out in front of me, as I watch the glowing ball of electricity grow in size and finally throw it at Tituba. It hits her square in the chest as she crumples to the ground. I start to let my shield down for just a second, when a bolt of electricity hits me in the back and brings me to my knees.

Madame Laveau walks around me, circling like a vulture.

"Well, my, my. Thank you for making this so easy for me Mae," she says as she walks over to Tituba, checking her pulse.

I thought it was going to be much harder than this, but you've served your sister up on a platter for me, and for that, I thank you," she says as a wicked smile crosses her face.

Madame Laveau grabs Tituba and lifts her up, taking a knife from the sheath around her thigh. With a brief incantation and the downing of an elixir, she takes the knife and slices Tituba's throat, blood pouring out everywhere. Madame Laveau drops Tituba's lifeless body onto the cold, hard ground and starts to laugh as I scream and scramble towards Tituba's body.

"I don't understand. I thought you were on her side. Why would you do this?" I ask her through sobs.

"Because my dear, there's only room for one Voodoo Queen in this world and that throne belongs to me," she replies.

Just then Tituba's amulet stone lights up a bright purple and explodes into a million tiny pieces, scattering into the wind.

"And now, so do her powers."

As I sit there holding Tituba's body in my arms, tears streaming down my face, Madame Laveau throws her arms up towards the sky and starts to chant in tongues.

The sky starts to darken, and the thunder intensifies, as the wind starts to pick up blowing as hard as a hurricane, when the Salem witches appear in the clearing, forming a circle around Tituba, myself, and Madame Laveau.

"It's time dear, you must let her go," Genevieve says.

"We need you right now Mae."

Genevieve was right, we had to stop her, or Salem was lost forever. I set Tituba's body down gently on the ground and got up, standing with Genevieve and the others, taking their hands in mine. The Salem witches begin to chant a spell of their own to counteract the dark magic at work, but the rest was up to me.

Madame Laveau begins to levitate mid-air, summoning the Powers of the Damned for herself, unaffected by the others or the fact that we've got her surrounded. I know the end is near and I have to act fast, but I'm so distraught over Tituba, I don't think I can do this, when suddenly my mother's words echo through my mind,

'Love is the key.'

Memories come flooding back of Tituba and I as children playing with dolls together, chasing each other through the woods, and reading our favorite stories together.

Tituba was my sister and I loved her, regardless of her betrayal. Then memories of my parents danced through my mind, followed by the memory of being named the coven's High Priestess. So much love fills my heart at that moment that I felt warm despite the freezing temperature outside.

I take one hand and press it to my amulet, thinking of all those fond memories, as swirling lights flickered from the Lapis stone.

Around the outside of the circle were the spirits of my ancestors, thousands of them, holding hands and joining in the chant. Just then an old spell came into my mind, and I know it is from my parents.

Without a second thought, I reconnect to the circle and begin to speak the words,

'Darkness falls on this night,

but we call upon the light,

vanquish this evil from time and space,

remove the evil from this place.'

Suddenly holes puncture through Madame Laveau's body, as light pours through the openings. She lets out a piercing scream as she explodes into a pile of ash, blowing into the wind. The dancing demons in the shadows flee as the sky begins to open up, revealing the sunshine beyond.

The Salem witches cheer and hug as the spirits of the ancestors disappear from which they came. Genevieve embraces me in the biggest hug of my life.

"I'm so sorry about Tituba dear," she says.

"Thank you, Genevieve, I know she's on the other side with the ancestors now, they'll guide her, and she'll be okay," I say through a smile.

Salem was safe, the threat was eliminated, and all was back in balance.

6 months later…

"Are you nervous Mae?" Genevieve asks me.

"Very. What if people don't like the changes I made to the shop?" I ask her.

"Are you kidding? This place is amazing. Twice the size as before and even more modern. They're going to love it. Especially the mural of our fallen witch sisters." she replied.

"Any word yet on the whereabouts of Papa Doc?" I ask her.

"Not yet, we've tracked him all over the world but as soon as we get close, he moves again. He's a sneaky one but don't worry Mae, we'll find him and banish him to the Underworld for eternity, where he belongs," Genevieve says.

"I'm sure we will. Okay, are we ready to open the doors?" I ask her.

"Ready when you are Mae," she replies.

I walk over to the front door, unlock the bolt, and turn the 'Closed' sign to 'Open' as a mass of people start to enter the shop.

"I want to welcome you all back to the re-grand opening of Spellbound," I say to them as they enter, greeting each person with a smile and a "welcome back.'

Everything was back to normal, and I was home again.

To Be Continued…

And stay tuned for a BONUS

story; Forged in Darkness.

A tale of Tituba's origin story.

Forged in Darkness
By Chelsea Allen

Chapter One

I looked down at my hands and they were covered in blood.

My mother's blood.

Her body lay lifeless, crumpled at my feet, and I was screaming. I'm not sure when I started, but I was finally aware that I'm screaming, tears rolled down my dirt-streaked face. People finally stopped their bustling to notice me and gathered around to see what the commotion is, when a gentleman picked me up and turned me away from my mother's body.

"Look at me," he said.

"It's okay, quiet down now. Take a deep breath, you're okay now," he continued.

He gently rubbed my back and carried me away, and that was the last time I would ever see my mother.

I was nine years old.

Doctor Porter and his family took me in like I was one of their birthed children. He was a prominent doctor in Salem and his family was well off because of his position within the community. They had a large multilevel colonial in the center of town and an older daughter named Mae.

She was thirteen and took me under her wing. Despite our different appearances, she never looked at me differently or treated me like I don't belong. She soon becomes my sister, my best friend, and I hers.

However, the Porters had a dangerous secret, one they decided to share with me when I turned ten. They were witches and ran a coven right here in Salem under the townsfolks noses.

I promised never to tell a soul. a promise I would one day break.

For the first few years, they taught me everything they knew about light magic, helping me practice spells and create potions even though I didn't have any actual powers.

It was fun to pretend and be one of them though, a connection I so desperately sought.

It wasn't until my thirteenth birthday that everything changed. I woke up that night around 3 am, drenched in sweat, my heart racing. I looked around the room and saw him, a shadow man dancing across my bedroom wall. I was terrified and tried my best to hide underneath the covers, but he pulled them back just enough to whisper in my ear.

"Don't you want to see your mother again Tituba?"

I was frozen in fear, and what felt like an eternity had passed before I answered him, but with a shaky voice I said, "Yes, I do," and I pulled the covers down to see the shadow man sitting at the foot of my bed, watching me.

"I can take you to her Tituba, you just need to take my hand," he said.

Without a second thought, I climbed out of bed and took the shadow man's hand and followed him into the darkness without ever looking back.

The Underworld was a dark and dreary place, full of caverns and lost souls. The smell of fire and brimstone burned itself deep into my nostrils, searing a memory I'd never forget. There was a faint glow of red as we walked down the beaten path, as the sound of chains and screams filled the air.

"What's that noise?" I asked him.

"Do not be afraid little one, for many surprises await you on this night," he replied.

We continued down the dirt path for what seemed like ages, when we finally came to a towering black wrought iron gate. Etched across the top of the gate was the word 'Underworld.' The shadow man merely took a bow and the heavy gate slowly groaned open.

Once it was clear, we stepped through the entrance and what lay before us was a lake of spewing hot lava. Surrounding both sides were hundreds of iron cages, strung magically from the top of the cave, and dropping into the lava at various intervals and back up again. However, these cages were not empty, as they held the bodies of those who sold their soul to the Devil, to spend an eternity in the pits of hell fire. The blood curling screams were unbearable, but I couldn't look away.

"This way little one," he called.

I'd fallen behind and ran to catch up to his side. As soon as I did, he had come to a stop in front of a throne, atop three blood covered steps steeped in shadow. It was no ordinary throne however, as this one was made entirely from the skulls of the damned. The shadow man took a knee and motioned for me to do the same. I was confused as to what we were doing kneeling before an empty throne when suddenly there was movement from the atop the shadows.

"My my, Papa Doc, what have you brought me today?" Madame Laveau asked in her sultry voice. She had that Creole accent that only Native's from New Orleans do.

Papa Doc replied, "Oh, I've brought you a treat Ms. Laveau, don't you worry."

There was something about the exchange that should have made me panic and flee for my life, but I felt comforted, almost like I was home, so I didn't dare ask any questions.

Madame Laveau slowly descended the stairs, the light hitting her face as she got closer to us. She was beautiful with her smooth chocolate skin and her hair pulled back into tightly wound braids. Her lips were painted blood red and her eyes as black as night. Her nails were long and came to a point, adorned black with red tips. Across her neck was an emerald green amulet, set into silver, hanging down low onto her chest. Her dress was long and black and had a train for what seemed like miles. It reminded me of a wedding dress almost. It was tight in the bodice and flowed from the knees down.

She truly was the most magnificent thing I'd ever seen in my life, and she oozed of power and darkness.

"Tituba, I presume?" she asked as she offered me her hand.

I nod.

"How do you know my name?" I asked her.

"Oh sweetie, everyone down here knows who you are. We've waited a long time for your arrival. Happy birthday by the way," she said to me.

"Who are you?" I asked

"Oh, forgive my manners darlin', I'm your Auntie Laveau and this is your Uncle Papa Doc and we're going to take great care of you." She replied.

"We've got much to teach you little one and your training starts tonight," said Papa Doc.

"Training for what?" I asked them.

"Oh, don't you know yet?" Madame Laveau said.

"You're a Santeria Voodoo Queen and you're going to be the strongest force this New World has ever seen. Darkness runs in your blood baby girl and your magic triggered tonight. Now come along dear, there's much to teach you before sunrise."

Chapter Two

When I awoke the next morning, I felt different; powerful and in control. I was no longer that orphaned little girl from the streets many years before, I was Tituba, Santeria Voodoo Queen and I would make others fear me.

I remember that first morning at breakfast clearly. Mrs. Porter had porridge served again for the fourth day in a row and I wanted something different. I had asked nicely at first for the cook to prepare me eggs and bacon, but she insisted we needed to finish off the porridge.

With a scream, I picked my bowl up and threw it against the wall, porridge running down the floral wallpaper. She let a brief moment of fear cross her face, before she put her hardened mask on and demanded I go to my room without breakfast. I got up from the table and stomped off up the stairs with a wicked smile upon my face, satisfied with my performance. Once I got up to my room, I locked the door behind me and conjured myself some eggs and bacon, just what I had asked for.

That afternoon when Mr. Porter got home from work, he heard about my outburst at the breakfast table and came up to my room to speak to me about it. The door was open, but I didn't want to talk to anyone. I was simply biding my time until sundown when Papa Doc would be back for me. When he knocked gently on the open door and started inside, I whipped around so fast and threw my hand out, slamming the door shut in his face from across the room.

I don't think he understood what had happened at first because he simply walked away. It wasn't until a few moments later that I heard Mr. and Mrs. Porter whispering from their bedroom about my behavior. I concentrated harder so I could hear them clearly and then I heard the world, 'abilities' get thrown around. It wouldn't be long now until they figured it out.

Once the sun went down, I sat on the edge of my bed and waited for Papa Doc to arrive to take me back to the darkness. Shadows danced across my bedroom walls, and I knew the demons were out to play, bringing him with them. Papa Doc didn't appear as a shadow man this time, instead he was human.

He had white paint covering his face, with black lines painted vertically. His eyes were painted in black rings and his lips were as black as night. He had long dreadlocks with various beads and feathers adorning them, with a black top hat to boot. There was a purple sash around the base of the hat, giving it a pop of color in all the darkness. He wore multiple rings on every finger, many with a skull emblem on them and his suit was a black and purple pinstripe to match the sash atop his hat. He walked with a cane and had a slight limp on his left side, though that certainly didn't indicate any sign of weakness on his part.

"Are you ready little one?" he asked me.

"Yes, let's go," I replied as I grabbed my books and headed for the shadow portal on my far wall.

Papa Doc grabbed my hand and led me through the portal, the dancing demons following behind us as the portal closed with a snap. This time we appeared at Auntie Laveau's house in New Orleans, right off the bayou. There were alligator heads hanging down from the roof, dusty mason jars covered the porch as a dim yellow porch light lit the entry way. An aged rocking chair adorned the porch adding a little charm to the dilapidated old shack of a house, and in its seat sat a voodoo doll with pins sticking out of it in all directions.

Fireflies lit up the swamp as crickets chirped nearby and above us was a full moon so big and yellow, and I could almost reach up and grab it from the sky. As we crossed the footbridge to get over the bayou, an alligator swam underneath, showing its white sharp teeth as it swam by, looking for its next meal. Papa Doc was a few steps ahead of me and knocked on the door with 3 loud taps and opened the door to let us inside.

It was dimly lit inside, but the shadow demons danced across the walls and ceiling to music I couldn't quite hear. The living room was filled with shelves of potions and mason jars with various body parts inside, both human and animal alike. There were cages hanging from the ceiling with chickens inside, and a large bookcase towards the back of the room with many leatherbound books, many in different languages, but based on the symbols that adorned them I knew they contained black magic.

Auntie Laveau entered from an adjoining room through a wall of hanging beads.

"Hello my sweet, you're right on time for dinner," she said.

"Isn't it a little late for dinner?" I asked her.

"Oh, not this dinner my dear. We have a surprise for you," she replied.

"Come child, take my hand and let's go sit down at the table. Because tonight, we feast."

I walked into the room, and it smelled of iron, the scent of blood. It's all over the walls, the floor, the ceiling, and I realized the room is painted in animal blood. There on the table was standing a large white goat, gnawing on some hay. He bleated and kicked at the table in fear.

Auntie Laveau walked up behind the goat and grabbed him by the belly, holding tightly while Papa Doc grabbed him by the horns and steadied him in place.

"Grab the knife little one," Papa Doc told me, nodding to the butcher knife on the table's edge.

"It's your time to join us Tituba and you must make a sacrifice to seal the bond," Auntie Laveau said.

It took me a few seconds before I understood what they wanted me to do. Slowly I grabbed the knife and walked over towards the goat, each step echoing in my head. This was my home, they were my family, and this is what I was meant to do.

I took the knife and ran it across the goats' neck with one

quick slice, and blood poured from the open wound, coating us

from head to toe. The goat tried to scream from the pain, but it

only bled more. It struggled to break free and kicked at the table,

but it was held in place by Auntie and Papa Doc.

After several minutes, the goat finally fell limp to the table,

twitching every once in a while, from its nervous system shutting

down. Blood continued to flow from its neck in what seemed like

buckets, until finally it ceased.

I took the knife and stabbed into the chest cavity, ripping

and tearing my way through the flesh, until I hit bone. I grabbed

the edges of the ribcage and with all my force I pulled them apart,

exposing the heart. I reached into the cavity and pulled the heart

out.

It was deep red and full of blood and was still warm as I

held it tightly in my hand. I admired the beauty of the organ as I

held it in the light, such beauty in the ability to hold life in my hands. I looked over to see Auntie and Papa Doc staring at me, studying me to see what my next move will be, when I take a bite out of the heart. Blood squirts all over me as I tore through the thick flesh, ripping pieces off and eating them like a Thanksgiving dinner.

Auntie and Papa Doc walk over to me and place their hands upon my shoulders, as Papa Doc says,

"You are initiated now little one, welcome home. What's ours is now yours, and what is yours is now ours. You shall never walk this Earth alone again, as long as the darkness is at your side."

Chapter Three

A rooster crows in the distance, alerting the townsfolk that a new day has arrived. The sky is illuminated with streaks of purple as the brightest orange fills the horizon, bursts of red within, looking like a wildfire ignited across the sky.

I step through the portal and back into my bedroom as it closes behind me with a snap. I look down and realize I'm still covered in blood. I walk over to the wash basin and rinse my face and hands as best as I can when I hear it, footsteps down the hall. I quickly jump into bed and pull the covers up to my chin and feign sleep, just as Mr. Porter opens the door.

"Tituba, it's time for church," he says. I roll over so I'm facing the wall and simply reply,

"No." I say it with such force and malevolence that he recoils at the word like he's just been bitten by a rattlesnake.

Without another word, he leaves the room and shuts the door behind him.

Once they finish breakfast, the Porters leave for church. I hear the front door close as I jump out of bed and head for the bathroom. I walk inside and untie the strings on my bloody nightgown, as it hits the floor at my feet. I stand before the clawfoot bathtub and close my eyes, my arms raised out in front me.

I start to chant an ancient tongue and slowly raise my arms higher as boiling water starts to fill the tub. Once the spell is complete, I step inside, the heat of the water so welcoming and relaxing. I lay myself back in the tub as the water starts to turn crimson red from the dried blood that adorns my body.

I clear my mind as I slip further and further into darkness as the dancing demons take me away. I'm lost in my mind for what seems like an eternity when there's a knock on the door. It's Mae.

"Tituba are you okay?" she asks. "You've been in there a long time."

I pull myself out of the tub and walk towards the door, dripping water all over the floor. I open the door and simply smirk at my dear sister, brushing past her as I walk to my bedroom, naked and dripping as the demons continue to dance around me.

Lunch is awkward as the Porters are taking turns staring at me, recoiling at every move I make.

"Tituba, are you feeling okay, you've been acting strange the last few days?" Mae asks me, breaking the silence that looms over the room.

At first, I stay silent, unsure of how to answer when finally, I reply,

"I'm fine Mae, I've finally found my home."

A confused look crosses her face as she looks over at her parents for confirmation. They are smiling and let out a little laugh, overjoyed to hear that I feel at home here. Little do they know I'm not talking about them, but I'll let them live in their safe little bubble a little while longer.

After lunch Mae finds me outside in the woods, laying amongst the fallen autumn leaves, looking up at the clouds.

She lays down next to me and grabs my hand and says,

"You know you're my sister Tituba, no matter what and I love you. I want you to feel like part of the family because you are, you're one of us and that will never change."

I'm taken aback by what Mae says and a strange flood of emotions overcome me. Mae has always had my back since the day they took me in. She's never treated me like I was different or unwanted. We would play with dolls together and hide and seek for hours on end. She was my best friend. However, the last few days have changed everything, and I had to choose between the light and dark magic and last night I made my choice and there's no going back.

A twinge of guilt hurts in deep in my heart for just a second and then it's gone.

I can't do this; I can't let myself get pulled back into the light.

I turn to Mae as I pull my hand away and say,

"I'll never be your sister Mae and this will never be my family," as I get up off the ground and turn to walk back to the house.

As the sun starts to set, I hear hushed whispers coming from Mr. and Mrs. Porters room.

"The cards are never wrong Tom. She's evil and she will be our demise if we don't stop her," Mrs. Porter says.

"She's only thirteen Anne, she's just a girl. We made a commitment when we took her in to take care of her and to protect her and that's what we need to do," he replies.

"There's something wrong with her Tom. Her behavior has changed, she's cruel and withdrawn and she's always in her room staring out the window. Ever since her birthday, she's become a different person," Mrs. Porter says.

"Then we must…," just as Mr. Porter is about to reveal his plan, my room goes dark and the demons dance across the walls.

Papa Doc comes through the portal with a snap and a wicked smile crosses my face.

"Are you ready little one?" he asks.

"More than ever," I reply as I take his hand and disappear into the darkness of the portal.

*   *   *   *   *

Anne lights the last candle and takes a seat across from her husband. They sit within a salt circle with a pentagram drawn on the wooden floor underneath them. Hundreds of white pillar candles fill the room and incense burn on a table nearby.

The room is dark except for the candlelight, casting shadows across the walls.

Anne and Tom join hands and began to chant in unison,

"Reveal to us what she hides,

in the darkness is where she resides,

bring us the answers that we seek,

show us what is hidden so deep."

White light swirls around the room, glimmering like diamonds in the sunlight wrapping around the Porters when suddenly their heads snap back, and their eyes turn white as snow. The room goes cold as ice and they begin their journey, lost within the trance.

The Porters awaken in a memory, Tituba's memory, in the Underworld. They see her being led down a path by a shadow man, past the pits of Hell Fire as the smell of smoke and sulfur fill their lungs. They follow them to the skull throne where Tituba meets Madame Laveau, and the shadow man reveals himself to be Papa Doc.

They hear Madame Laveau tell her she is of Santeria Voodoo descent when suddenly the memory changes, they're at a shack in the bayou, watching Madame Laveau and Papa Doc hold down a goat, while Tituba slits the innocent animal's throat. It's when Tituba cuts the heart out and eats it, that the Porters are shocked awake, back to reality in their living room.

"Oh my God Tom, she has chosen the darkness. She's initiated! We're too late," Anne cries out with tears streaming down her face.

"Her magic must have remained dormant all this time, until her thirteenth birthday, when Papa Doc came for her. We had no idea she had powers Anne; we couldn't have done anything to save her. Her future was written before we ever even brought her into this house. It's in her blood; the darkest of magic the world has ever seen," Tom says.

"What do we do now Tom? We can't pretend that we don't know what she is or what she's capable of. We have to protect ourselves and protect Mae from her," she says.

"We must act as if everything is normal, but we'll cast protection spells tonight on Mae, the staff, and on ourselves. From now on, we'll give Tituba her space, we'll keep her inside, and we'll isolate her from other people as much as possible. It's key to keep her happy and not anger her, as her magic is new and she's not yet in control of it," he says.

"We'll be okay Anne. Once she's of age we can get her out of the house but until then she's our responsibility and we must keep our family and the people of Salem safe from her."

Anne cries into his shoulder as Tom hugs her tight, fear churning deep in his stomach. He would never let Anne know but he is scared, and it is a fear so seeded that he began to think he will never sleep again.

Tituba must be stopped at all costs, but this is his daughter he is talking about. The dirty little girl he picked up off the street that day her mother was murdered. The little girl he bought dresses for and countless dolls and celebrated years of birthdays with.

A daughter he would read to every night before bed, one he taught light magic too and the secrets of the family. His little girl was evil now and he feared her more than he loved her.

Chapter Four

I am at Auntie's house when I felt it, like an icepick through the ear, the pain overtakes me and knocks me off balance. I drop the book in my hands and immediately grab my head, willing the pain to stop when flashes of memory came flooding to the surface when I see their faces, clear as day.

The Porters were in my head, and they knew who I was and what I had done. Suddenly the pain stops as fast as it had started and I drop my hands to my side, letting out a sigh of relief, but that relief quickly turned to rage as I threw my fists down on the table and let out a piercing scream.

The lights begin to flicker, and the room begins to shake. Books fly off the shelves from around the room and potion bottles and mason jars burst into glass shards. Loose papers blow around the room in an invisible breeze and even the dancing demons take shelter within the shadows. Blood begins to trickle out of my ears, running down the side of my face when everything stops abruptly and goes quiet. Auntie is standing in the doorway with her right hand raised in the air and a look of satisfaction upon her face.

"My, my, what rage you have buried deep inside of you my dear," she says.

"I'm sorry Auntie, I don't know what happened, I just…" I say when she grabs my shoulder and turns me to face her.

"It's okay, little one. You have much to be angry about and what you just did is very advanced for your skill level. You are quite strong my dear, but you still have much to learn. Now let's clean this blood off your face and get back to your studies," she says.

"What about the mess I made?" I ask her.

"What mess my dear?" she replies as I turn around to face the room and see that everything is back to as it was before my tantrum, like it never even happened.

Magic.

As I settle down to continue reading about the history of black magic, I can't help but wonder about my history and where I originate from.

"Auntie, where do I come from?" I ask her.

"Well, my sweet, you hail from the Yoruba tribe in West Africa. They are an ancient tribe that have practiced the black art of Santeria for many centuries. Most of their rites include sacrifices, both animal and human alike, ensuring their offering to the Gods guarantees them protection and a wealthy harvest, among other things," she says.

"Would you like to meet them, little one?" she asks me.

"How?" I ask her.

"Follow me little one," she says holding out her hand.

I take her by the hand, and we walk over to her alter, adorned with animal skulls and various bottled liquids. She opens her grimoire, and the pages start to flip by themselves, coming to a stop on a certain page. Auntie begins to chant in tongues, when I look over and see a portal opening on the far wall. It's black as night but larger than life, consuming everything along that wall. Suddenly it goes quiet, and Auntie pulls my hand, leading me towards the portal and together we jump inside. The portal closes behind us with a loud snap and everything in the room is back as it should be.

When we step out of the portal, it's pitch black out, and thousands of stars dress the night sky above us. In the distance is a bonfire, raging into the sky, fire licking the atmosphere like it's burning the moon above. I can hear the beating of drums and chanting of voices as I see people dancing around the fire, adorned in animal skins and colorful fabrics.

A lion roars so fiercely that birds take off from the trees next to us, flying to their next destination. Just then, the squealing of a warthog catches my attention. The tribes people are holding it down as an elder is speaking in tongues and holding a large blade up to the moonlight. His eyes are glazed over to snow white as he appears to be seeing things that we cannot. Once he completes his chant, he walks over to the warthog, bends down next to it, and slices its throat so deep that its head is barely hanging on anymore. Blood squirts out of the wound, coating the elder and the tribes people, many who are still dancing around the fire while others are bathing in the blood of the animal and chanting in unison.

Auntie leads me towards the tribe, each step vibrating with anticipation. As we close the gap between us and the tribe, the elder turns and looks upon us, as if he's been expecting this moment. As we reach the elder, Auntie takes a knee before him, showing her respect for him and his power.

I start to kneel when he grabs me and says, "The Queen does not bow down to anyone."

"How did you know?" I ask him.

"I am the elder," he replies, "I can see all; the past, the present, and the future. And I've been expecting you for some time Tituba."

The elder leads me and Auntie to a secluded hut a little way away from the bonfire where everyone dances and celebrates. Once inside the hut, the elder gestures for us to sit around the small fire that warms the middle of the room. The elder walks to a table on the other side of the hut and pours a liquid into a cup. As he walks towards me, he chants a few words and waves his hand over the cup, handing it to me.

"Drink this Tituba and all questions will be answered," he says. The drink is green and smells putrid but the elder stares at me, waiting, and I knew I couldn't resist. I took a deep breath and slam the drink back as fast as possible, doing everything in my power not to be sick, when suddenly the room starts to spin, and everything goes dark.

*   *   *   *   *

In a secluded area under the light of the full moon, there are several midwives tending to a freshly labored mother as she holds her crying newborn tightly in her arms. The mother is singing to the child in a hushed tone, trying to calm the infant down as the midwives work faster to stop the bleeding. After several minutes, the mother starts to fade away, a soft song still upon her lips.

It is then that the word 'Tituba' escape her lips as she finally succumbs to death.

The midwives take the infant from the mother's arms and continue to sing the song in unison as they walked the babe to the elders hut, unsure of its fate.

The elder looks the infant over, ultimately deciding to use it as a sacrifice in the next ritual on the full moon, as orphaned children have no place in the tribe. It is then that one of the midwives protested with such force that the elder was taken by surprise at the display of defiance and disrespect.

Her name is Viola.

Viola stands up for the infant, putting her own life on the line in place of the babe. Confused as to why this particular child,

Viola simply replies that she has a feeling in her bones. After much deliberation, the elder grants Viola the infant and charges her with the responsibility of caring for it until it grows of age.

*   *   *   *   *

When Tituba is five, the elder reads her stories of the ancestors and of the great prophecy that he believes she would one day set in motion.

He tells her of a great and powerful darkness that would be 'born' where even the demons would dance at her feet. She would be initiated by the most powerful beings and be the strongest force of evil the world has ever seen. The day would come when a great battle between light and dark would ensue and the darkness would consume the light, snuffing out all the goodness in the world.

All the pain and hatred would be unleashed out into the world to consume everyone it touched, ultimately plunging the world into Hell where she would rule as Queen.

*   *   *   *   *

As Tituba grows older, Viola grows more fearful for her. The elder is grooming her to fulfill the prophecy and that would mean Hell on Earth and that scares Viola. It isn't until Tituba turns nine that Viola devises a plan to get her out of Africa and to the states where she would be safe and away from the tribe. Viola drugs Tituba late one night and sneaks down to the docks, carrying Tituba in her arms.

When she arrives, she sneaks them both inside a wooden crate, destined for a cargo ship to the states the next morning. As the crate is loaded onto the ship, Viola knows this is a betrayal to the tribe punishable by death, but she also knows she would be giving Tituba a chance at a better life, a life in the light away from the darkness.

The journey is long and rough, and Viola has to keep Tituba drugged the entire time, for fear she would give their hiding place away. After several weeks on the water, stuck inside the wooden crate with just the water and food Viola was able to carry that night, the ship made port in Salem. She waits until the ship empties its crew and passengers to break open the crate, using every ounce of force she has left. Viola crawls out of the crate, wincing at the sunlight, unable to fully open her eyes, and Tituba begins to stir awake.

Viola grabs Tituba and picks her up, carrying her in her arms. She struggles to stand, and walking was even harder after being folded up inside that box, but she is determined to get off that ship and onto land. Viola walks off the ship carrying Tituba in her arms, making her way through the crowds and into the market, when she felt it, a force so dark she knew the elder had located her and sent a demon to do his bidding.

Viola tries to run as fast as she can, looking behind her as she ran, but unable to see anything or anyone there. When suddenly, a knife plunges deep into her belly, as she drops to the ground on her knees, blood pouring from her stomach. She sets Tituba down and crumped to the ground at her feet, dying as Tituba starts to scream, unsure of what was going on or where she even was.

That is when Dr. Porter picks her up and saves her from the horrible scene, although in Tituba's mind, her adoptive mother got what she deserved. Afterall, she had taken her from her home and kept her drugged for weeks. If Tituba could've, she would have killed Viola herself for her treachery.

*　　　*　　　*　　　*　　　*

As I finally wake up, I look around the hut to see Auntie and the elder sitting around the fire, watching me, waiting.

"How was your journey Tituba?" the elder asks me.

"Did you see what you needed to see?" he adds.

"It was you," I say.

"When I was a little girl, you would tell me of a dark prophecy. It's about me, isn't it?" I ask him.

"Yes Tituba, you are the one we have been waiting so long for. Africa was your home, and the Yoruba tribe was your family," he says.

"We've gone through great lengths to protect you over the years and ensure that you chose the correct side on your thirteenth birthday Tituba. You are destined for great things, and you must start preparing," he adds.

"Thank you elder for taking me on this journey. I think I finally understand and I'm ready to embrace my heritage and bring the prophecy to fruition," I say.

He gives me a nod and Auntie takes my hand in hers. "Are you ready to go little one?" she asks me.

"Oh yes Auntie, we've got a lot of work to do," I say as a wicked smile crosses my face.

Chapter Five

I appear through the portal in my bedroom just before daybreak, as the dancing demons frolicked in the shadows. The Porters discovered my secret, that I had been initiated into darkness, embracing my heritage to fulfill the dark prophecy, becoming the most malevolent force the world has ever seen.

I could smell the sage they used to cleanse the house, sense the protection spells they cast and feel the force of the runes radiating throughout the house, but their powers are no match for me. It is like a pinprick on my skin, annoying but nothing fatal.

I knew the Porters would do everything in their power to keep me locked up, isolated from Salem and away from the community. Its' protection is their priority at all costs, and they aren't going to let anything stand in the way of that.

They eventually move me from my second-floor bedroom to the basement, where it is dark and damp, but it is private and all mines. I spend most days asleep, biding my time until the sun set, and the shadows fell, when the portal would open, and I can go home.

I spend my nights in the Underworld studying with Auntie and Papa Doc, practicing dark spells, magical combat, and potion making. The Porters would tell anyone that asked about my whereabouts that I took ill and must remain inside the home.

No one questions the good doctor, and in time everyone forgets about me, but I never forget who I truly am.

4 Years Later….

The Porters grow increasingly wary of me over the passing years, ensuring to maintain as little contact as possible. My food is delivered by a dumbwaiter and if a member of the staff had to come down for anything, they made sure it is a volunteer.

I often question why I am still alive and living freely in their home, but I already know the answer to that. They don't possess the power to destroy me or bind my Voodoo magic and without the ability to overpower me, they let me fly under the radar.

As long as I am not hurting the people of Salem, they won't have to start a war they can't win.

Luckily for them, my interest isn't in the townsfolk, but in fulfilling the dark prophecy predicted so many centuries before. I am only seventeen and already becoming the most powerful being the world has ever seen. I study and practice my magic all day, perfecting spells and creating potions, ensuring that the Santeria tribe's traditions are continued through my practice. Every full moon, I sacrifice an animal, eating the heart and bathing in the blood as an offering to the Gods.

Every night I escape Salem and head home to the Underworld where Auntie and Papa Doc wait for my arrival. They test my knowledge and my magic to ensure I am performing where I should be, pushing me to dig deeper and go darker. There is nothing I can't do, and I am unstoppable.

One night, we venture to New Orleans, where the demons dance to the finest Jazz. The moon above is like a glowing ember of fire in the sky, illuminating everything on the street with the utmost brilliance. The city is bustling with tourists, the chatter so loud it could make your head spin. Auntie, Papa Doc and I head to Auntie's Voodoo shop on Main Street to mingle amongst the tourists and find the weakest of the bunch, for we have a youth spell to cast and need a human sacrifice.

As we make our way down Main Street to the shop, we can't help but smell the ripeness in the air, the very smell of innocence and purity. It is intoxicating and we were getting drunk. We come to a large store front with the name *'Madame Laveau; Voodoo Priestess'* lettered across the front window.

You can feel the evil and darkness oozing out of every corner of the shop before you even step inside, making it a haven for the locals and a gag shop for a handful of tourists.

Tourists come in wanting love potions and revenge spells and other frivolous items, not even knowing what it was they were truly searching for in life, never knowing their purpose, only to be concerned with utter nonsense. As we open the door to the shop, the distinct smell of purity wafted out and we know the perfect sacrifice is inside.

Auntie enters first and approached the customer who stood in the corner of the shop, looking at jars filled with various liquids and animal parts. Auntie has this ease about her that could make the devil himself feel calm and at peace, so as she comes up behind him, the customer doesn't think twice to be concerned. Auntie has a knife in her right hand and as she stands behind the young man, she brings her arm up and slit his throat in one fluid motion.

Papa Doc locks the door behind me as I start to chant in tongues. Slowly he joins in the chant as Auntie drags the bloody, lifeless body over to the center of the room where we stand. The lights around the room flicker and die as the floorboards begin to shake revealing a red light shining through the cracks, illuminating the entire room while the dancing demons take to the shadows.

As we continue to chant, Auntie starts to cut the heart out of the young man, blood pouring out all over the floor beneath us. Finally, she gets through the rib cage and reaches in, pulling the heart out of the chest, bringing it up to her mouth and taking a bite, blood squirting out all over her face and soaking her magnificent outfit.

We each take turns eating the heart while drawing runes on our skin in blood to complete the youth spell, giving us each another year of life. With the last bite, the lights come back on in the shop and the red lights from the floorboards disappear, everything returning to normal.

This becomes a tradition for us every year to return to Auntie's shop in order to complete our youth ritual, offering a sacrifice to the Gods, ensuring our life for one more year.

In the beginning it was more for Auntie and Papa Doc, but as the years turn into decades, and the decades into centuries, it becomes a necessity for me as well.

3 years later...

On my twentieth birthday, Mae is named the Coven's High Priestess. Over the years, she took to her studies and truly became a fierce competitor. The little girl I once knew, whom I called my sister, I now called my enemy. She represents the light, the goodness, the very thing that could destroy me and prevent the prophecy from coming to fruition, and there was no way I am going to let that happen. Mae has to be stopped at all costs, even if that means killing her.

In the Summer of 1692, the Salem Witch Trials begins when Reverend Cotton Mather creates a mass hysteria on false claims, which are then 'validated' by bored, insolent children running amuck in the community, taking their revenge out on those they don't like. Many are falsely accused, but many more are prosecuted despite being innocent.

Due to the fact that I have been isolated at home for seven years along with the rumors the staff created about seeing dancing demons and hearing strange noises from my room, the butchered family cat, and lack of evidence of an illness, the townsfolk grow suspicious, and I am ultimately accused of witchcraft. I however use this to my advantage.

I decide that in order to kill two birds with one stone, I will give up Mae in exchange for my freedom, so I break my promise to the Porters and go to the Mayor with Mae's grimoire. He recoils at the sheer look of the book, praying with every turn of the page as he looks over spells and potion recipes, personal journal entries and family photos.

There is no mistaking who this grimoire belongs too, and Mae's fate is sealed.

The mayor releases me, and I take off into the woods, where I will portal to the Underworld come sundown. The Porters will notice my absence, but I don't care, I did what I had to do, and I have no regrets.

The next morning is Mae's trial and I make it back just in time to give my testimony and present the grimoire and its contents. I can't help but look upon the faces of the Porters as I speak to see the look of shock and utter betrayal looking back at me, but I feel nothing. After my testimony, I retreat back to the woods to await sundown, when Mae will be executed.

The hours feel like days, just dragging on in what feels like an endless loop. As the sun begins to set, I slowly make my way through the thick forest, back towards town. As I turn at the bridge

down by the river, I can hear the commotion as they bring Mae out

of the cells, tying her to the stake and building the pyre around her.

I snake my way around the corner of the courthouse, as the

dancing demons cast shadows across the walls when I hear the

mayor begin to speak.

"Mae Isobel Porter, you have been found guilty of

witchcraft and are sentenced to die by fire. Do you have any last

words?" he asks her.

Mae remains silent and defiant as he finally says,

"Then may God have mercy upon your soul."

The mayor lights the pyre, setting it ablaze as I walk into

the crowd of onlookers just in eyeshot of Mae and shoot her that

wicked smile of mine, for I have finally won.

It is seconds later, right before the stake was engulfed in

flames, that I notice a sudden chill in the air with the distinct

presence of magic. I can feel it pricking upon my skin, like hundreds of ants taking a bite out of me, when I see it, Mae's lips are moving, and she is casting a spell.

Before I can counteract her magic, the pyre is engulfed in bright flames and all I can hear is Mae's screams.

I am too late.

I run towards the woods before any of the townsfolk can identify me, cursing under my breath the entire time. Mae cast a reincarnation spell, I can still taste it on my tongue, and I am angry that I didn't see it coming.

As I came to a clearing, I stop to catch my breath and glance around me. There is nothing. No movement, no life whatsoever, I am completely alone.

All I know is that I have to get back to the Underworld, to my home, because as far as Salem knows, I am as dead as my sister if they ever find me.

I quickly chant a few words as a portal opens mid-air with a loud snap and I jump inside, knowing that one day I will be back for my revenge.

Made in the USA
Columbia, SC
17 July 2022

63596437R00098